PUFFIN BOOKS

THE MOUSE BUTCHER

On the still air from the distant fields came a horrible mixture of a roar and a scream with a snarl mixed in, and even at that distance it was so loud that everyone knew one thing for certain. It was the noise of no ordinary creature!

Somewhere in the green leafy depths of Hobbs' Hole there lurked a monster – or so the legend ran. There were tales of ghosts, and mother cats frightened naughty kittens with threats of the creature of the marl-pit. The island's cats steered well clear of Hobbs' Hole and the monster never came out.

But then young Tom Plug, the butcher's cat and a fearless mouser, ventures into Hobbs' Hole on a heroic mission – a mission that could easily cost him his life . . .

The extraordinary story of Tom's encounter with the monster is fast and furious, and continues in the tradition of Dick King-Smith's other highly popular books.

Dick King-Smith was a farmer in Gloucestershire for many years, and this background has proved invaluable for his amusing animal stories. He then taught in a village primary school for several years, and now writes full time. He has recently become well known for television appearances with his miniature wire-haired dachshund, Dodo, on TV-am's *Rub-a-Dub-Tub*. His novel *The Sheep Pig* was a winner of the Guardian Children's Fiction Award.

Other books by Dick King-Smith

ACE
DAGGIE DOGFOOT
DODOS ARE FOREVER!
THE FOXBUSTERS
HARRY'S MAD
MAGNUS POWERMOUSE
MARTIN'S MICE
NOAH'S BROTHER
PADDY'S POT OF GOLD
PETS FOR KEEPS
THE QUEEN'S NOSE
SADDLEBOTTOM
THE SHEEP-PIG
THE TOBY MAN
TUMBLEWEED

COUNTRY WATCH
TOWN WATCH
WATER WATCH

For younger readers

BLESSY AND DUMPLING
GEORGE SPEAKS
THE HODGEHEG

Dick King-Smith

THE MOUSE BUTCHER

Illustrated by Wendy Smith

PUFFIN BOOKS

PUFFIN BOOKS

Published by the Penguin Group
Penguin Books Ltd, 27 Wrights Lane, London W8 5TZ, England
Penguin Books USA Inc., 375 Hudson Street, New York, New York 10014, USA
Penguin Books Australia Ltd, Ringwood, Victoria, Australia
Penguin Books Canada Ltd, 10 Alcorn Avenue, Toronto, Ontario, Canada M4V 3B2
Penguin Books (NZ) Ltd, 182–190 Wairau Road, Auckland 10, New Zealand

Penguin Books Ltd, Registered Offices: Harmondsworth, Middlesex, England

First published by Victor Gollancz 1981
Published in Puffin Books 1983

Reprinted by arrangement with Viking Penguin, a division of Penguin Books USA, Inc.
Printed in USA
10 9 8 7 6 5 4 3 2 1

CONTENTS

CHAPTER I

The Butcher and the Doctor

The fittest animals, as everyone knows, stand the best chance of survival. And the mouse that poked his face out of the tumble-down shed at the back of the deserted butcher's shop was very fit indeed. He could run faster and squeak louder and eat quicker than the rest of his tribe, and his eyes and his ears were as sharp as his nose.

Alas, he was proud of his powers, and pride, as everyone knows, comes before a fall. If only he had run straight from the shed into one of the grass-tunnels in the matted ruin of a lawn, if only he hadn't stopped to arrange his whiskers, if only a precious second had not gone by while he said to himself, "I am the greatest."

But the pause and the preening and the pride made that precious second his last. Black death dropped from the top of the broken garden wall and white teeth cut off his final squeak.

Tom Plug was very black. He wasn't particularly big but he was sleek and muscular. Short-haired, green-eyed, sharp-clawed, he looked what he was—a hunter. Unlike most cats, he did not play with his victim. That first bite killed it, and now he split and gutted it with professional skill. His strong jaws made short work of the meal, and soon the tail and back legs were all that was left of the greatest mouse.

Later that morning, Tom lay upon the bare marble slab in the window of the empty shop and gazed down the deserted village street. There were gaping holes in some roofs where tiles had been blown off, paintwork everywhere was drab and peeling, and gardens were wildly overgrown and choked with weeds and tall grasses. Outside, above the shop-front, the faded lettering still read, *Percy J. Plug. Pork Butcher*, but it was more than twelve moons now since Tom had last seen the man; the remains of his blue-striped apron and his straw hat still hung behind the door, but the mice had dealt hardly with them. The once scrubbed and scoured surfaces of the heavy wooden tables bore nothing but mouse-dirt and snail-trails, the brown stains on the rows of knives and cleavers and saws were not of blood but of rust, and from the big steel hooks in the ceiling hung only spiders' webs.

Opposite Tom lay his elderly friend Giglamps Macdonald, once the doctor's cat. He had long ginger fur, a white bib and paws, and, curiously, white rings like spectacles around his yellow eyes.

In the old days doctor and butcher had only met

when one needed meat or the other medicine, and their cats had not met at all. But one morning not long after the humans had gone, Tom Plug, swinging along the village street with a mouse in his mouth, had noticed a ginger-and-white cat sitting outside a front door with a discoloured brass plate set in it. *Dr I. Macdonald MD MRCP*, it said. Tom could not read this, but he could read the hungry look on the ginger cat's face and on an impulse he dropped the mouse on the pavement in front of him. So their friendship had been born.

*

Tom stuck out a foreleg to its fullest extent. He spread his toes, unsheathed his claws, and regarded them thoughtfully.

"Mmmmmmm," he said, "nice here in the sun. But it won't get us lunch. While I'm away the mice will play. Or we might have rat. Or sparrow. What d'you fancy, Giglamps?"

"Chuck steak, laddie," said Giglamps in a faraway voice, "finely chopped, with a small piece of calf's liver on the side." He ran his tongue neatly over the end of his nose.

"Or perhaps a little cod. Lightly steamed. With just the hint of a cheese sauce. And a saucer of Gold Top."

"You've been dreaming," said Tom.

"Och, it's staring up the street that does it, laddie," said Giglamps, yawning. "I can still see it just as it was. Humans everywhere. With their shopping baskets. Catering for our needs. Ah, humans! They were useful creatures to keep, you know. They've been gone a long time."

The two friends lay silent, remembering those strange days. Usually no more than a handful of people visited the island in the season, but suddenly, over a couple of days, a great fleet of boats had come from the mainland, boats of every size and kind, boats crammed with frightened, worried humans to swell the island's population from fifty or sixty to a thousand. They remembered how the grocer had run out of tinned food, and the baker of bread, and the greengrocer of fruit and vegetables, and the Colonel of patience, and the Vicar of hope. Every last pig, bullock, cow, calf, sheep, horse even, had made its way through Percy J. Plug's slaughterhouse and down one or another of a thousand throats. Until at last there was no meat on the island for humans to eat.

"And then that great ship came," said Tom, picking up the other's train of thought as cats can.

"That's right," said Giglamps, "and they all had to wade out, among the rocks, carrying their bairns."

"Took their dogs of course."

"Stupid beasties, actually seemed to like swimming."

"I wasn't going to get my feet wet."

"Nor I."

Gradually, as time passed after the going of the humans, the cats of the island had dropped into the habit of assuming amongst themselves their late owners' titles. The head of the cat family up at the Big House, for example, was always addressed as "Colonel Bampton-Bush", the seniors at the island's three farms as "Farmer Truebody", "Farmer Goodfellow" and "Farmer Sturdy", and the patriarch in the old rambling house beside the church was of course "Vicar" to all. Only Tom used Giglamps' private name. To the rest he was "Doctor".

As for Tom himself, the island cats spoke of him as

"the Mouse Butcher". It was a long time, after all, since the walls of Percy J. Plug's slaughterhouse had rung to the squeal of a dying pig, so that this title seemed right. Certainly the mice thought so, those that were left.

"What was it all about, d'you suppose?" Tom said.

"I don't know, laddie," said Giglamps. "I doubt we shall ever know. They were funny creatures, humans, you see. Always fighting. Always falling out, one lot with another lot. Many a time in the old days I've lain in the Doctor's room and listened to him and the Colonel and the Vicar discussing the strange habits of the human race."

"Why did they fight?"

"Och, didn't like each other's ways. Often wanted to take the other lot's land."

Tom looked shocked. "Take over territory that wasn't theirs?" he said.

Giglamps nodded. "They didn't seem to have any proper rules of behaviour like we do," he said. "About the only thing they were any good at was providing food on time," and he looked sideways at his young friend.

The Mouse Butcher took the hint and jumped off the marble slab on to the dusty floor in one beautiful black sinuous movement. He slipped through the cat-flap (squeaky now for want of oil) in the back door of the shop, and padded soundlessly away down the weedy path through the wild garden.

Some minutes later, as he lay in ambush beside a runway, his eyes, ears, nose and muscles were all concentrated on the mouse to come, but his mind was running on the recent conversation. Fancy humans coveting each other's territory! No self-respecting cat would dream of such a thing!

Though I wouldn't mind a change from mice, he thought.

CHAPTER 2

Enter the Colonel

It was a simple four-course lunch. It was mouse for starters, with mouse to follow, then mouse, and mouse to finish. As always, Tom laid the four corpses neatly upon the marble slab in the window of the butcher's shop. It was as though he was impelled to in memory of Percy J. Plug, who had always so carefully arranged cutlet and chop, sirloin and brisket, liver and kidneys to catch the eye of the passer-by.

As they were about to begin, Tom saw that there was indeed a passer-by, both of whose great golden eyes were firmly caught by the sight of the outstretched mice.

"Who's the hungry-looking geezer outside?" he said.

"Geezer?" said Giglamps with a low purr of laughter. "Good job he can't hear you. Frightfully posh chap that, you know. Persian. Pedigree as long as your tail."

"Funny," said Tom, "I've never seen him before."

"Well you wouldn't have, with all due respect, laddie," said Giglamps. "That's the Colonel. From up at the Big House. There's quite a few of them up there. That's the head of the family, Bertram Bampton-Bush. Never seen him down in the village before, they've always kept themselves very much to themselves."

"You'd have thought the humans who used to live there would have taken them along," Tom said. "Pampered variety like that."

"Och well, it was a curious set-up at the Big House," said Giglamps. "The cats belonged to the old fellow there but his wife had a lot of dogs, little fluffy yappy things. And no doubt he was told to save the dogs and leave the cats."

"Told?" said Tom. "D'you mean he just tamely did whatever his wife said?"

"Och yes, that's the way with a lot of humans. You'd not have been surprised if you'd known her. Her word was law. She was a Lady, daughter of a Duke."

Tom had no idea what a Duke was, but he felt quite sure no wife of his should ever push him around like

that. He looked again at the figure outside the window.

"Poor fellow," he said. "He looks ever so ribby."

"Yes, well, they're probably finding it hard going," said Giglamps. "Always been spoon-fed, y'know. Never had to fend for themselves."

"That reminds me," said Tom, straight-faced, "do start, please. I hope two will be enough for you?"

At the end of lunch, there only remained four pairs of back legs and four tails.

Outside the Colonel sat still, seemingly hypnotised by the scene within. His coat was a beautiful smoky blue, the colour of lavender in a cottage garden, but it was harsh and staring.

Tom was a kind-hearted animal and it worried him to see a handsome cat in such a condition.

"I think I'll have a word with him," he said. "I might be able to help him."

"Suit yourself," said Giglamps, "but he'll probably snub you. He's a very toffee-nosed fellow."

What I mean is, he thought to himself, he's quality and you're common, good friend though you are. He belched quietly and yawned.

"Anyway, Tom, I must get home. Lot of work to do. I've got mice in the dispensary."

"Of course," said Tom, "I know how conscientious you are about keeping things as they used to be."

What I mean is, he thought to himself, old Doctor

Macdonald would probably have been fast asleep in his armchair by this time in the afternoon, and that's just where you're going, lazybones, good friend though you are.

After the squeak of the cat-flap had announced Giglamps' departure, Tom neatly picked up the remains of the meal and made his way out. He turned round the side of the shop and walked up the narrow alleyway that separated it from the bakery next door. He came out on to the village street and dropped the legs and tails into the gutter. He sat for a moment, cleaning his nose and lips with the side of one forepaw and considering how to address such a very important Persian.

He was saved the trouble however, for the blue cat called out to him in a high and haughty voice, "One moment, my good cat. I'd like a word with you."

Stuck-up beast, thought Tom, and he got up and walked, slowly and deliberately, towards the other, his ears pricked, his tail high, his green eyes fixed on a spot somewhere just above the blue head.

There was no actual threat in the manner of his approach but for all that it made the Colonel uncomfortable. Maybe it was Tom's appearance, sleek, fit, hard-muscled, but at all events the blue back arched a little, the blue tail fluffed out, and the high voice climbed a fraction higher.

"Now look here, I don't want any nonsense from

you, my good cat," said the Persian in a slightly trembly tone.

"I haven't any nonsense to offer you," said Tom pleasantly, and he stopped a yard away and sat down.

"Now look here," said the other, "you don't seem to know who I am."

"Haven't a clue."

"Well, I'm Bampton-Bush. Bertram Bampton-Bush."

"Plug," said Tom.

"Now look here, Plug," said Bertram Bampton-Bush, "I just happened to notice you, er, lunching with Macdonald. Decent enough sort of animal in his way. You seemed to be providing the food. I take it he employs you, what?"

Just as I thought, said Tom to himself, he's half starved for all his airs and graces. There could be something in this for me.

"We have an arrangement," he said. "After all, gentlecats can't be expected to do their own hunting the way we common fellows do."

"Well, I'd hardly call Macdonald a . . ."

"Especially," interrupted Tom, "a real aristocat like yourself. Sir," he added quietly. A quick glance from the green eyes saw the golden ones widen in pleasure and the flat snub-nosed face look even more self-satisfied.

"Ah. Quite," said Bertram. "Well. Now look

here, Plug my good cat. I think I can see my way, as a special favour to you that is, to putting a little business in your path. How would you like to supply me and my family, up at the Big House?"

Tom was not prepared to allow the Persian to believe that Giglamps was his only "customer".

"I'm a busy cat, you know, Colonel Bampton-Bush," he said. "I have a great many calls on my time. Catering for you would mean my taking on extra help. I imagine you have a large family?"

"I have a wife," said Bertram. "And about a dozen children or more."

"Exactly," said Tom. "And you're probably thinking of a daily delivery?"

"Certainly," said Bertram. "You see, Plug, it's not simply a case of people of my sort not caring much for working-cats' pursuits. Mousing. Ratting. That sort of thing. All right for some, I dare say. And as you rightly remark, one is used to being fed on a decent dish with decent food from the fridge. But it's not simply that."

"What then?" said Tom, though he knew the answer.

"Well, the fact is, Plug, that the humans were extremely wasteful creatures, always dropping bits of food under tables and leaving it around on plates in cupboards and chucking it to their damned dogs. And since they left, there's been no waste food in the Big

House. So the mice and rats have left too. There's nothing for us to eat."

Oh yes there is, thought Tom. Out in the country-side, where the last corn crops re-germinate and the root crops still sit in the ground and the wild fruits and berries drop—there's food for a million rodents and birds, animals that any cat worth his salt can go and catch for himself. You may not be worth your salt, Colonel B-B, but perhaps you could be useful to me. I'm not saying I want to take over your territory like humans apparently do, he thought. But I wouldn't mind a good look round it.

"I quite understand, sir," he said smoothly. "I'm sure we can work something out. Can you think of anything you might care to give me in return for my services? For example, if you have sources of food supply up there not available to common or garden cats, I could perhaps contract to butcher them for you and your family on the understanding that I should receive a proportion for my own use?"

The golden eyes glinted in the flat face. "Now look here, Plug," said Bertram Bampton-Bush, "I believe you're on to something there. I mean, one doesn't actually go out on to the estate, you know—too damned muddy and brambly—but one of my sons is pally with young Tibby Truebody down at the Home Farm—boys will be boys, y'know—and she told him that the place is thick with pheasant and partridge.

And of course, there are quite a lot of rabbits. And hares. If you can catch them. Ha ha."

"Ha ha," said Tom, and the green eyes glinted in the sharp face.

There was more talk and a meeting at the Big House was arranged for the next day. Then they made their good-byes.

Once Tom was out of sight, he doubled back and watched from hiding. And as he watched, the high and mighty Colonel Bertram, head of the family of Bampton-Bush, lord of the Big House, the aristocat of the island, looked hastily around him, crept quickly forward and bolted the legs and tails. He peered around again, and then drew himself to his full height and with the dignity of centuries of good breeding, set off up the village street to the Big House.

CHAPTER 3

Hobbs' Hole

Almost in the middle of the island was a huge deep pit, perhaps the size of a football stadium. Over centuries men had made it, digging there for red marl to spread upon their fields. But for the last hundred years, it had fallen out of use and become overgrown, not just with thick undergrowth and scrub but with tall trees. Their tops were now level with the rim of the marl-pit, so that a watcher on the edge would have looked down into a great sea of greenery at every level.

The islanders had called it Hobbs' Hole, for an old poacher named Billy Hobbs had once lived there in a hut of sticks and corrugated iron and sacks. Billy Hobbs and his hut were long gone, but Hobbs' Hole was as full of wild things as it had been in his day. In the middle of it was a hollow oak tree. And in the middle of the tree sat the wildest thing of all.

At first sight you would have thought this creature too big to be a cat, and at second glance too hideous, for what he gained in size was balanced by a saga of losses. One ear was in tatters, the other almost gone. He had but one eye, and an injury to his great round face had pulled up one side of his mouth in a permanent snarl. A trap had removed all the toes from one forefoot. His tail was a stump.

This was Great Mog.

Great Mog was a feral cat, a cat gone wild. He had been born in the village, the only surviving child of a thin half-starved female who belonged to nobody in particular. She had taken to stealing to support herself and her kitten. Principally she hung about Percy J. Plug's shop and it was here one day that the incident occurred which was to alter the shape of both Great Mog's life and his person.

One afternoon when he was about two months old, Mog accompanied his mother to the butcher's shop. She waited in the alleyway between it and the bakery, her anxious pointed head poking around the corner to watch for a suitable moment, while behind her the tabby tom-kitten fidgeted impatiently.

When at last they reached the door the shop was empty of people but full of the heavenly smell of meat. The mother made for a string of sausages upon the slab, the child for a clutch of kidneys on one of the tables, when out from the back room came the butcher, cleaver in hand, dog at heel! The young Mog's last sight of his wretched mother was of her frantic fleeing form barely a cat's length in front of the yellow lurcher's long jaws, before he turned to see the butcher towering above him, arm upraised. Down

24

whistled the shining cleaver, thudding into the scoured surface of the wooden table, and then Percy J. Plug had his shop to himself again.

But between the pork chops and the pigs' kidneys lay three tabby inches of kitten tail.

And so out into the wild went the orphan Mog, to learn to hunt and to kill and to survive. By some freak of heredity, his bob-tailed body grew to giant size, and with it, as traps and shot-guns and dogs made their contributions to his looks, grew his hatred of all living things. All his memories made the outlaw bitter, but especially the memory of that day in the butcher's shop.

On this particular evening Great Mog sat in his leafy nest in the crown of the hollow tree and looked about him. You could not say his ears were pricked—there was not enough of them—but he was listening intently to the noises in Hobbs' Hole. He had nothing to fear, since men and their dogs were gone, but he had a territory to protect, for the marl-pit was his, and his alone. Between it and the village and farms was a kind of no-cat's-land, where others might hunt if they wished but woe betide them if they were rash enough to enter the Hole. Once, two cats from an outlying farm had indeed ventured in, but they did not live to regret their rashness. Great Mog killed them both, and the magpies and the ants cleaned up.

But strangely there was one cat that had the right of entry, perhaps because he was of use to the great wild tabby, perhaps because he was so mean and insignificant in appearance. He was a very thin small brown cat, so small he could have walked under Great Mog's belly had he been fool enough. His pointed face and slanting almond eyes came from some Siamese ancestor. He was quick, and servile, and cunning. His name was Creep.

This evening Great Mog could hear a whole orchestra of sounds. Above and around him were the noises of bird-song and animal scamperings. He heard the slow rustle of a foraging hedgehog, the grunts of badgers coming out of their sett deep in the red marl, the pattering footsteps of a fox passing beneath the hollow tree on his way out to the night's hunting.

Great Mog stretched and yawned and was just

about to climb down from his nest when a thin nasal voice made him spin round.

"Evenin', Captain," said Creep. "Hope I didn't startle you." Great Mog's expression could not change, for his snarl was fixed, but his one eye flashed and the stump of his tail twitched.

"Damn you, Creep," he spat. "Told you a dozen times. Don't come in upwind. Bad for my nerves."

"Nerves, Captain?" said Creep. "Why, you 'aven't got a nerve in that whole magnificent body of yours. Ain't nothing on this island could scare you." He crouched very flat, ready for instant flight, his slit-eyes fixed on the monster above.

Great Mog came down from his tree, a little awkwardly because of the missing claws on his fore-foot. He sat on his haunches with his back to the little brown cat and combed his ragged ears with his good paw.

"Well?" he said. "What d'you want? Eh?"

"Want, Captain? Me, Captain?" whined Creep. "Why, just the pleasure of settin' eyes on you . . ."

"Get on with it," cut in Great Mog, in a low growl.

They knew each other well, these two, hated each other but used each other. The one valued his right of entry to Hobbs' Hole and the status it gave him in the eyes of the rest of the island's cats. They did not know exactly what it was that lived in those green leafy depths, but there were tales of ghosts, and mother cats frightened naughty kittens with threats of the monster of the marl-pit. All gave Creep a wide berth. The other relied upon him for news of anything and everything that might go on in the outside world, that is to say in the island outside Hobbs' Hole. Quick, silent, small, cunning, Creep was the perfect spy.

He saw the twitching stump and tensed himself for flight should the wild cat's temper boil over, as it often did.

"Sorry Captain," he said hastily. "It was just something I saw today. In the village. Thought it might interest you."

"Men?" said Mog quickly. "Are men back?"

"Niaouw!" said Creep. "Niaouw, nothing like that, Captain. It was just two cats having a chat."

"What's funny about that?"

"One of them was the Colonel."

"Down in the village?" said Mog. "I thought you told me that chicken-and-cream lot never went outside the Big House?"

"Exactly," said Creep, "but there he was. All skin and bone, too. Eating rubbish out of the gutter."

"Who was the other then?"

Now Creep knew everything about everything. He knew how Great Mog had lost both mother and tail. All right, he thought, the man and his dog have been gone for ages but there's a black cat living in the old shop, the Mouse Butcher they call him. Can't even have been born when old grumbleguts here got the chop but that won't matter. Let's have some fun. Let's stir up some trouble. Let's see if we can make the fur fly!

"The other one, Captain?" he said. "Oh, that was the cat from the butcher's shop."

"Butcher's shop?" said Great Mog very softly, and his one eye flashed and his stump began to twitch.

"Oh, didn't you know?" said Creep carelessly. "There's a black cat lives in the shop. Tom Plug his name is but everyone calls him the Mouse Butcher."

"The Mouse Butcher," said Mog in a kind of thick whisper. "Did he belong to . . . that man?" His stump fluttered madly.

"Yes."

A listener might have thought there was at least one great dog left upon the island, such was the deep growling that mingled with the bird-song in Hobbs' Hole. At last it died away, and Great Mog spoke again, still quietly.

"What were they saying?" he asked. "Could you hear?"

"Niaouw, Captain," said Creep. "I couldn't get close enough."

"Find out," said Great Mog. "And now get out."

And as Creep made his silent way up the steep side of the pit he heard beneath him the horrid rasping noise of Great Mog sharpening the claws of his good foot on the hollow tree.

CHAPTER 4

Diana

The morning after his meeting with Bertram
Bampton-Bush, Tom Plug made his way, as
arranged, to the Big House. Like all cats, he was
intensely curious, and he could hardly wait to set foot
in those spacious grounds where, in the old days, he
would never have dreamed of going. So he arrived
extremely early, and, finding no one about, allowed
himself the luxury of a good look round. He toured
the walled kitchen garden, a jungle of weeds now,
and searched the long dry greenhouses, empty save
for the skeletons of dead chrysanthemums. Then he
slipped through a broken door set in the wall and
across the tall grasses of what had been a sweep of
lawn to the once formal gardens.

There was a pattern of symmetrical flower beds—
now covered in groundsel and dandelions—triangles,
diamonds, oblongs, quarter-circles, each bounded by
a ragged hedge of box. In the centre of this pattern
was a large round pond. Pausing to lap, Tom could see
below his reflection a number of huge golden fish,
moving slowly among the water-lily stems.

Suddenly he felt that he was being watched and
looked quickly up at the dozen or so square eyes that

were the front windows of the Big House. They were blank—or was that a movement at the corner of one of them?

Next instant there was the most terrible blood-chilling shriek behind him that laid Tom's black ears flat and set every nerve in him a-jangle. Tail held straight out behind him, he shot across the grass-grown gravel paths and in through the first window that offered, while behind him a peacock strolled majestically down for his morning drink.

As Tom lay breathless on the floor of the room into which he had burst he heard someone giggling—or the nearest a cat can get to a giggle, a kind of soft purr with a hiccup in it—behind a dusty sofa. And in a moment there walked out from behind it the most beautiful creature Tom had ever seen. Scarcely more than a kitten, she had the flattest face, the blackest nose, the dearest little whiskers, the most glorious golden eyes, and her coat—her long soft exquisite coat—was the most wonderful shade of the most wonderful blue that Tom could possibly have imagined in the world, a world turned instantly into Paradise.

Walking forward—in, of course, the most un-believably elegant way—she sat down in front of the black intruder, and the gold eyes looked directly into the green.

"You're a very fast runner," said this vision of

beauty—in a voice like cream and treacle mixed.

Tom gulped.

"Got to keep fit," he growled awkwardly.

"You look *very* fit," she said. "By the way, introduce yourself."

"Tom," said Tom. "I mean my name's Tom Plug. The Mouse Butcher."

"Oh," said the vision. "Sorry. I'm Diana. Diana Bampton-Bush. I live here. So I think you'd better tell me what you want, Mr Tom Plug."

"I've got an appointment," said Tom. "To see your . . ." He was just going to say "father" when it occurred to him that she might possibly be not a daughter but—oh horrors!—a very young wife. He became thoroughly confused.

"To see, er, Colonel Bampton," he said, "that is, I mean, Colonel Bertram-Bush."

Diana's golden eyes positively twinkled.

"You want to see Daddy?" she said.

Tom heaved a huge inward sigh of relief. "Yes," he said. "Yes, please, miss."

"Oh for goodness sake!" she said. "Call me Di. Everybody does. Except Mummy."

Tom was too bewitched to ask what Mummy called her, but the answer came that very instant. From the depths of the house came a loud commanding voice echoing along the lengthy corridors and around the high-ceilinged rooms.

"Di-*ah*-na!" it cried. "Di-*ah*-na!"

Then suddenly the room filled with Blue Persians, youngsters of Diana's age, perhaps her litter-mates, and a number of young adults, a dozen or more in all. They crouched or sat, and stared unblinkingly at the black stranger. And then through them swept the figure of Lady Maud. Like her husband's, her coat was dull and matted. Round her scrawny neck was

the tattered remnant of a red silk bow, and she was painfully thin.

Behind her came Bertram, and it was easy to see that the parents had been giving almost all the food they could find to their family, at their own expense.

"Di-ah-na," said Lady Maud. "Who, pray, is this, ah, visitah?"

"This is Mr Plug, Mummy," said Diana quickly. "The Mouse Butcher."

"Butchah?" said Lady Maud, on a rising note.

"Yes, he's come to see Daddy on business."

"On business? To see your Fathah? There must be some errah."

"No, no, Di is quite right, my dear," said Bertram hastily in a placatory voice. "Come along Plug, my good fellow, come into my study and we'll have a chat," and he turned and went hastily out of the room and along a corridor.

Tom hesitated before the baleful stare of the lady of the house, but Di gave him a little tap with one adorably rounded paw. "Go on, Tom," she whispered, and Tom, his mind reeling at the touch and the sound of his name on her lips, pushed his way through the serried Persian ranks and followed the Colonel.

The deal was soon struck. Bertram Bampton-Bush was no business cat. Tom was. Bertram was a soft touch. Tom a hard nut. Bertram was half-starved, as was his wife, and as his family soon would be he feared, unless someone could be found with the strength and skills to provide for them. Tom, it seemed, was that someone, and Bertram gave in to every condition that Tom set.

"I shall need a free run over your entire estate, Colonel Bampton-Bush," said Tom.

"Yes."

"That freedom of entry to apply to any cats I may have working for me."

"Yes, yes."

"In return I will contract to provide you and your family with the choicest available foodstuffs, all you can possibly eat."

Bertram passed his tongue rapidly around his lips. "Very well, Plug."

"And over and above that," said Tom, "I shall be entitled to the balance of all kills for my own use. As I seem to remember, you agreed to this at our first meeting?"

"A proportion, I think you said, Plug."

"The balance."

"Oh, very well."

Tom thought quickly. If I'm to see Di regularly, he said to himself, I must have the right of access to the Big House so that we can meet often. He had no intention of revealing the reason for his final demand, either to Bertram then or to Giglamps in conversation later, but like a boxer who sees his opponent reeling, he decided to go for the knock-out blow.

"One last thing, sir," he said. "If I'm to serve you properly I must have a room in your house for my own use."

Bertram gulped. "My wife . . ." he began.

But Tom went easily on, "You see, there's little point in my having to take your family's share, the very choicest as I said, all the way down to my shop in the village and then bring it back here again, now is there? I mean, far more convenient for you if I butchered it here—you'll want it all properly prepared of course, a gentlecat like you."

Bertram gulped again. "I'm not sure that my wife would be, will . . ."

"I do hope you'll see your way to agreeing to this last point, sir," interrupted Tom sweetly. "Otherwise . . ."

"No, no, Plug," said Bertram hastily, "certainly . . . you must have a room . . . Can see that . . . The, er, servants' quarters . . . Er, self-contained little wing . . . Sure you wouldn't mind, good fellow like you . . .? My wife . . ." He finished lamely, his eyes filled with pleading.

"Of course, sir," said Tom. "The servants' quarters will do admirably."

Nine, ten, out! he said to himself.

CHAPTER 5

Pheasant for Supper

Giglamps heard all this later that evening, after supper. They had shared a pheasant.

"He was just strolling down the drive as I left the Big House," Tom said. "Practically walked into my mouth. They're not used to being hunted you see."

Giglamps cleaned his face delicately, belched luxuriously and settled himself comfortably in the deep leather armchair.

"Mah–vellous!" he said. "Pah–fectly mah–vellous!"

"That's it!" chuckled Tom. "That's Lady Maud's voice exactly! How did you know?"

"Oh well, I have met her, laddie. Once. In the old days. Doctor Macdonald used to go up to the Big House quite regularly to play some card game with Colonel and Lady B–B and the Vicar. On one occasion I followed him and slipped in, uninvited. Never again though."

"Why, what happened?"

"Well, I think old Bertram was prepared to be civil, you know, offer me a small saucer of milk, that sort of thing. He's a stuffy old snob, but basically kind-hearted. But her Ladyship wasn't having any of it.

"I remember she was lying in front of a fire in one of the smaller rooms, looking absolutely magnificent, one must say, with a brilliant red silk bow tied round her neck. And when her husband had introduced me she looked not at me but straight through me, and said in that awful braying voice, 'Some othah time, perhaps, Bertie. It's very neahly time for dinnah, and you're not dressed yet. I'm sure Mr, ah, Macdonald can find his own way out.' And off I went like a cuffed kitten."

There was a long easy silence while the two friends lay contentedly in a brilliant sea of black and bronze and green and red feathers, thinking pleasant thoughts.

At last Giglamps belched once more and said, "That was a meal and a half, Tom. Get some of that into Bertram and Lady Maud and in a little while they'll give you anything you want."

A vision rose before Tom's eyes—a vision with the flattest face, the blackest nose, the dearest little whiskers, the most glorious golden eyes.

"I hope they will, Gig," he said. "I hope they will."

CHAPTER 6

At the Churchyard

Tom spent the night at Giglamps' house. Breakfast next morning was less luxurious, just a couple of sparrows.

"Sorry," Tom said after an early hunt, "that's all I could find. Anyway a bird in the hand . . ."

". . . is worth two in the Bampton-Bush," said Giglamps. "Ha ha."

Giglamps licked his lips, brushed his whiskers out, left, right, and regarded his friend straightly. "I can see what's in it for you," he said. "Good hunting and the best of grub. But it'll be hard work, you know. All the killing, the carrying, the butchering. You're going to need help."

"Oh thanks, Giglamps, that's decent of you."

"What? No, no, I mean expert help."

Tom scratched his head with one hindpaw. "Well, I don't know where I'm going to get it. The farm cats are too far out, and as for the village cats, who is there? You tell me. There's half a dozen cottage cats, and that old pair from the pub, Rose and Crown, but not a decent hunter amongst them. Talk about pulling down a pheasant or a hare, most of them must have their work cut out to catch a mouse! When all's said and done, 'Mouse is the staff of life'! As Ecclesiastes would say," he added.

They looked at each other.

"That's your cat, laddie!" said Giglamps, grinning as though he'd come straight from Cheshire.

"Of course! Of course! That's it!" cried Tom excitedly, "Ecclesiastes and his family. The most expert specialist mousers on the island. If it's patience that's wanted, they've got it, especially that boy Job."

Ecclesiastes' family was numerous and as poor as the church-mice they lived on.

"Look," said Giglamps. "Why don't I go down and have a word with Ecclesiastes? I mean he's an old friend of mine, whereas I think you hardly know him?"

"You mean he's *your* sort of cat," said Tom with a smile, "and I'm a bit common."

"No no," said Giglamps. "Of course not."

"Well, I don't like to put you to all that trouble," said Tom. "Walking all the way down to the Vicarage" (it was a good two hundred yards), "straight after breakfast."

"You mean you're young and active," said Giglamps with a smile, "and I'm a fat old lazybones."

"No no," said Tom. "Of course not."

*

Giglamps went straight to the churchyard. It was a fine morning, and he found what he had expected. By almost every grave, it seemed, there lurked a cat. They were of all sizes, and of all colours, but they had in common a certain look, a kind of tired resignation to a life of hard work and small rewards. Still as the statues of angels and cherubim above them, the innumerable family of Ecclesiastes waited, by headstone and by footstone, by monument and memorial, for fortune to give them that day their daily mouse.

Giglamps, puffing a little from the unaccustomed exercise, rested a moment in the long grass, looking all about him for the head of the family. Eventually, espying a sudden movement beneath a great yew tree in a distant corner, he trotted down and found the

patriarch, his paws together in an attitude of prayer, and between them an extremely small shrew.

"Morning Vicar," said Giglamps. "Caught you red-handed, eh? How about the sixth commandment, then?"

He always said this and always Ecclesiastes made the same reply.

"Needs must, my dear Doctor," he said, "when the Devil drives." Mercifully, he ended the shrew's feeble struggles with one quick bite, and rose to his feet.

Ecclesiastes was a tall thin cat of mournful appearance, dark grey, with a broad collar of white fur around his neck. His sole wealth lay in his voice which was rich and rounded and resonant.

"Dear friend," he boomed, "tell me, I pray, to what happy chance do I owe the undoubted pleasure of your company?"

"'Happy chance' is right," said Giglamps and he proceeded to explain Tom's need for assistance in his new venture.

"I suggested this approach to you and your family, Ecclesiastes," he concluded, "because you are such expert hunters and because there are, if you'll forgive me, so many of you. How many are there, in fact?"

"A multitude," said Ecclesiastes. "Sometimes, if you in turn, dear friend, will forgive me, providing for them seems to necessitate as great a miracle as the

Feeding of the Five Thousand. In fact, not counting myself or my dear wife, who has remained at the Vicarage with the seven latest arrivals, there are a score and ten of us at work here this morning. It is the habit of my family, as I think you know, to choose our children's names from the books of the Old Testament, but at the rate of increase with which we are blessed, we shall soon be using the New."

"All the more reason," said Giglamps, "for Tom's offer to be of interest to you."

"Verily," said Ecclesiastes. "Let us repair to the Vicarage. I must, in all things, consult my wife."

They made their soft-footed way between the moss-covered tombs and the weatherworn gravestones, the only movements beside their own a number of sudden pounces from one or other of Ecclesiastes' silent, watchful children. At each the patriarch voiced his approval, lowering his voice to a mere purr.

"Well done, Leviticus," he murmured. "Oh, neatly, neatly, Habbakuk! See, a bold jump from Exodus! (An outgoing boy that," he whispered proudly to Giglamps.) "Ah, Lamentations has missed. How sad."

Inside the Vicarage, cold and damp even in such weather, they found Ecclesiastes' wife, a tubby tabby person, surrounded by a cluster of tumbling kittens. Unlike the rest of her family and despite the trials and tribulations of a life of penury and thirty-seven children, she gave an impression of comfortable jolliness. Her name was Genesis.

"So you see, my dear," finished Ecclesiastes, after a short sermon, "it appears that, thanks to Mr Plug's offer, we may look forward to better times."

"Land of milk and honey," said Giglamps.

"Super!" said Genesis. "Simply super! Really most frightfully grateful to you, Doctor. Be such a change. So jolly fed up with always eating the same thing."

Ecclesiastes threw back his head and raised his fine voice. "Cat shall not live by mouse alone!" he cried.

CHAPTER 7

A Good Breakfast

That evening, Tom and Giglamps compared notes, after supper, of course. Cats, unlike humans, never talk with their mouths full, so they shared a fat wood-pigeon before settling down on the butcher's marble slab. Giglamps related his morning's work.

"Fine," said Tom absently. "That's fine." He began to purr loudly, a faraway look in his eyes.

"Well?" asked Giglamps.

"Well what?"

"How did you get on? What sort of day have you had? You look as though you've eaten the cream."

"What? Oh, sorry. Yes, um, well I went up to the Big House. Had a conducted tour of the estate in fact."

"Conducted tour?"

"Yes."

"Who conducted you? Bertram?"

"No, matter of fact, it was that kid."

"Kid?"

"That kid I was telling you about last night. One of Bertram's daughters."

"Oh, Diana?" Giglamps said.

"Yes, Diana."

Giglamps stared hard at Tom and shut one eye. Tom looked away.

"Tell me all about it laddie," said Giglamps. So Tom told him about it. But not quite all.

He had arrived at the Big House in a more dignified manner than on the previous day. He stalked up the drive and climbed a great flight of stone steps to the massive front door, still ajar as the humans had left it in their dash for the rescue ship. Tom slipped through. The Bampton-Bushes were at breakfast, seated on the long refectory table in the dining-room. Bertram crouched at the head, Lady Maud at the foot, and the younger members were distributed between them. There didn't seem to be much for them to break their fast upon. Old rat it looked and smelt like to Tom, and Bertram and his wife ate nothing.

Tom crept away unnoticed and made his way to the fish-pond. He had never before employed his fishing technique on anything bigger than a tiddler and the fish in this pond were golden orfe, great monsters weighing two pounds apiece. But he didn't see why it shouldn't work. He crawled flat to the rim and turning his face sideways, very carefully dipped the end of a whisker into the water, making a little ring upon the smooth surface. Then he pulled his head back against his shoulders like a tortoise with-

drawing into its shell. Lazily, curiously, up swam a big gold shape. Swiftly, accurately, a black paw slipped under it and flipped it out. Helplessly, breath- lessly, the lord of the pond flopped and jumped upon the weed-grown gravel till one quick bite settled the matter.

The family were about to get down from the table when Tom reappeared, his head held high against the weight of the big fish, its body dragging between his widespread forelegs. The knowledge that Diana was watching—he only had eyes for her—lent him super-feline strength so that with a mighty effort he leapt upon the table with his burden, and laid it before Lady Maud.

"Your breakfast, my lady," he said. To Bertram he said, "Sorry I'm late, sir. Hadn't realised you were quite such early risers."

Bertram's golden eyes shone. "Damn good show, Plug," he said. And to his wife, "Shall I carve, my dear?"

"Allow me," said Tom, and he split and cleaned the fish with lightning speed. Ten minutes later there

wasn't even a scale to be seen. Lady Maud broke the satisfied silence.

"Nevah," she said distinctly, "nevah have I enjoyed a bettah breakfast. Children, you may leave the table," and when the family had gone, she turned and looked directly at Tom.

"Mistah, ah, Plug," she said. "To what do we owe this generous behaviah?"

"It's a little arrangement, my dear," said Bertram hastily, "between Plug and myself. He has undertaken to see to our catering henceforward."

"And in return?" said Lady Maud.

"In return? Er, well he is to have a percentage of the kills for himself, and er, a few friends. And . . ." His voice trailed off.

"And?" said Lady Maud loudly.

"Colonel Bampton-Bush is kindly letting me have the run of the servants' quarters, your ladyship," said Tom quickly. "So that I can prepare the day's menu —after consultation with you, of course—on the spot."

"Servants' quartahs?" said Lady Maud. "Day's menu?"

There was a short silence.

"An excellent ideah. How clevah of you, Bertie," said Lady Maud Bampton-Bush and, her aristocatic stomach filled for the first time in many moons, she lay flat upon it and began to purr.

CHAPTER 8

Conducted Tour

After breakfast Diana showed Tom around.

They started with the servants' quarters. There was a nice cosy sitting-room with a big comfortable armchair full of mice-nibbled cushions. Tom caught himself thinking the chair was just a nice size for two cats to cuddle up in. And next door was a store-room, half pantry, half larder, dark and cool with a huge stone slab running along the length of it on one side and flyproof, perforated zinc still intact over the window.

"This is where the humans used to keep a lot of their grub, I believe," said Diana. "Daddy was telling me about it last night. After I'd wheedled out of him just what your 'business' was all about. So I thought this would be a pretty good place for you to store your kills. There's a passageway here, you see," she bounced along in front, "that leads straight into the main part of the house. So that'd be convenient for you to bring stuff in for Mummy and Daddy and the rest of us. And convenient for me to come and see you sometimes, Mr Tom Plug. If I've got nothing better to do."

Tom's senses reeled.

"Incidentally," she went on, "that fish was smashing. Are we really going to eat as well as that from now on?"

"Better, I hope."

"I think I could get to like you. In fact I do like you. D'you like me, Tom?" Tom gulped.

"Yes," he muttered.

"I've got a name," she said.

He gulped again.

"Yes, Di," he said in a strangled voice.

They toured the whole of the Big House, whence the last mouse had long since fled, the stables and the other outbuildings, home only to a few ancient rats, and the gardens. These last looked more promising, for in addition to the golden orfe in the pond, Tom noted signs of many low-nesting birds, saw molehills in the ruined lawns, heard frogs in what had once been an ornamental stream, and put up woodpigeons in the tangle of the kitchen garden.

But it was when they got out on to the estate, the thick matted ungrazed pastures, the corn grounds unharvested but continually reseeding themselves, the fields of roots unpulled and potatoes undug, the overgrown woods, that Tom realised what a hunter's paradise were the lands of the Bampton-Bushes. Rabbits, hares, pheasant, partridge—they were all there just as Tibby Truebody had said. And they were there in their dozens and hundreds. The foxes and the stoats and weasels of the island did their best, but with man and dog gone, the balance was disturbed, and the game flourished almost unchecked.

Hardly were they through the first gateway than Tom killed a brood of young partridges. He suddenly realised that he had had no breakfast, and Diana had no objection to a second one, so they settled down to polish off the little ones.

"The humans used to shoot these, you know," said Tom. "These, and pheasants, and lots of things."

"Shoot?" said Diana, with her mouth full. "Wass tha' mean?"

"They had long sticks which went off with a bang when they pointed them, and the birds fell down."

Diana wiped her black lips with one blue paw, a gesture which Tom found utterly bewitching. "Funny things they must have been, humans," she said.

"Funny to think you've never seen one," said Tom.

"I've seen pictures of them," she said. "At home, there are lots of pictures with shiny fronts and silvery outsides. Seems to me they were silly little things. Mostly not much bigger than a mouse standing on its hindlegs. And some of them only had heads, no bodies at all."

Tom had never seen the silver-framed photographs in the drawing-room of the Big House but he knew

about humans and was beginning to explain to Diana that she'd got it all wrong because . . . when he looked round to find she was halfway down the field, leaping and skipping through the flower-filled grasses and batting at the bees and the brilliant butterflies, a prettier picture than any clumsy great human.

By the end of the tour, Diana was still filled with boundless energy and Tom with unquestioning adoration, but on quite a number of creatures the summer sun had ceased to shine forever. As well as the mother partridge, a selection of bodies had been cached along the way. There were half a dozen young rabbits who had cut it too fine, several fat fieldmice who had left it too late, and a black velvet mole who had risen above his station.

"Let's see," said Tom, "there are fourteen of you, aren't there? That should be enough for the day."

"Look, Tom," Diana said (he needed no invitation to look at her), "you're a marvellous hunter" (his tail shot up with pride), "and you work like a beaver" (he purred with pleasure), "but how are you going to keep this up, three meals a day, seven days a week, not just killing for all of us, but carrying the stuff home?"

"Ah," said Tom. "My friend Giglamps Macdonald and I have planned all that." And he went on to explain how the Vicar and his huge family of dedicated painstaking hunters would come the very next day, to reinforce his efforts in the feeding of the Bampton-Bushes.

"Yes, but don't you see," Diana said, "don't you see, you silly old Tom Plug, that the more hunters you have, the more kills they make, and so the more there is to carry? What we're going to need is a gang of porters. And I know just the ones."

"Who?" said Tom.

"My four oldest brothers," she said. "It'll do them a power of good. All they ever do is sit about grooming their coats and admiring each other's whiskers and making catty little jokes in Persian."

"But will they do it?" asked Tom.

"They'll do just what Mummy tells them," said Diana. "And Mummy will do just what I ask her to. Because I'm her favourite."

Oh, and you're my favourite too, thought Tom.

"So let's just take a couple of rabbits now, and then while you're preparing them, I'll bring the boys out here and they can pick up the rest and cart it back. Why, who knows, they might even get some mud between their toes and some brambles in their beautiful coats," and she turned a neat somersault of happiness at the thought.

The rest of the day was spent in the collection of the caches, the plucking and flaying and splitting and cleaning, and the serving of a magnificent four-course meal. The Bampton-Bushes were loud in their praise of Tom's skills, and even the newly conscripted porters forgot their sulks in the ecstasy of the blowout.

Later Tom and Diana went for a walk, and on the way back, coming in through the gardens, had happened upon a woodpigeon.

"And very tasty he was, laddie," said Giglamps at the end of Tom's account. "You seem to have had quite a day. Everything's going your way, huh?"

He stared at Tom and shut one eye again.

But Tom didn't appear to notice. His own eyes were narrow and his tail waved a little.

"There is one other thing," he said. "When we were at the far end of the estate, this afternoon, I suddenly realised that we must be very near Hobbs' Hole. In fact we were right at the edge of it. And then I suddenly saw these paw marks, cat's paw marks. I didn't say anything to Diana and I don't think she noticed."

"Well?"

"Whatever made them had lost the toes of one foot."

"Well?"

"The *size* of them, Gig," said Tom Plug in a hoarse whisper, "the *size* of them. I put my paw inside one of the marks and it was like a tea-cup in a saucer. I swear they were three times as big as mine."

"Did you see anything?" asked Giglamps, the hair rising along his back and his tail fluffing out like a bottle-brush.

"I didn't wait, I can tell you."

"Brrrrr!" said Giglamps. "Then they're right when they say there's a Monster in the Hole?"

"Yes," said Tom. "And they're wrong when they say he never leaves it."

CHAPTER 9

Creep Piles It On

"Well?" snarled Great Mog out of the corner of his mouth. A week had passed without sign of the spy, a week spent in brooding thoughts, thoughts as black as the object of them. Increasingly, the Monster found that he could not get the Mouse Butcher out of his twisted mind. He sat now in his nest in the crown of the hollow tree and looked down at the little brown cat whose sudden noiseless appearance had startled him out of a daydream of bloody revenge.

Crouching in his usual servile attitude, Creep squinted upwards. You great ugly ignorant bad-tempered freak, he thought to himself, you just wait till you hear what I've got to tell you, you'll go out of your tiny mind, you will. Talk about putting the cat among the pigeons, there'll be some feathers flying before I've finished. Someone's going to need more than nine lives. He put on his whiniest voice.

"Sorry I haven't dropped in lately, Captain," he said. "There's been so much going on . . ." He paused, and began to scratch one pointed ear with a back foot. He could feel the curiosity and frustration and anger almost shaking the tree above him.

"Damn you, Creep," spat Great Mog. "Tell me what's happening or I'll break your rotten back."

"All right, all right, Captain," cried Creep, "keep your hair on! What you've got of it, you mangy old muckheap," he muttered under his breath.

Great Mog's jaws began to open slowly, showing his huge yellow incisors, and Creep, reckoning him to be ready to explode, lit the fuse.

"It's the black one," he hissed, "the Mouse Butcher, you know Captain, him I was telling you about. He's got in with the Colonel and his family, he has. Got the hunting rights over the estate, got the Vicar and all his hundreds of kids working for him. What a time they're having! Pheasant, partridge, woodpigeon, hares, great golden fish—kill, kill, kill all day long. Even got the Persians to carry the stuff back to the Big House. Oh, and that's another thing—he's actually got his own rooms there, the black one has. Colonel and his lady all over him they are, can't do enough for him now he's filling their bellies. Why, he's actually courting one of their daughters, lovely little bit of fluff. He's some cat, that Mouse Butcher, he really is. Good-looking, great organiser, fantastic hunter—he must be the most talented cat on the island!"

Creep paused for breath, then went on, softly and reflectively, "Why, the way he's going on, Captain, he'll be doing a bit of hunting down here in the Hole before long."

There was such a horrible expression on Great Mog's already hideous face that Creep wondered if he'd overdone it. In fact, he'd done it just right, just as he had hoped. Everything that he had said had touched a-nerve.

Everything Tom had, Mog had not. Tom was handsome. Mog was hideous. Tom was popular, Mog a bogeycat. Tom slept in a fine house, Mog in a nest of dirty sticks. Tom lived on the fat of the land, Mog on what little a crippled cat could catch.

And finally Tom had love, the love of another cat, something that Great Mog had only had for a few short weeks from his poor thin mother until that dreadful day when . . . And at that instant all that store of hatred crystallised in the Monster's maddened mind. He would kill the Mouse Butcher if it was the last thing he did. He would leave the Hole and find him and kill him. Then he would be the king of the island, live in the Big House, feed on the finest food, marry the Colonel's daughter.

He came down from the hollow tree and began to strop his claws on its scarred bark while Creep slid hastily to one side. "Mouse Butcher!" said Great Mog between his teeth. "By the time I've finished with him, they'll be calling me Cat Butcher!"

"Going to teach him a lesson, then, Captain, are you?" said Creep, and when there was no answer, "How're you going to catch him then? He's very fast, you know. Moves like lightning."

Even in his madness, Great Mog realised the problem. Once he could get to grips, no cat—few dogs indeed, he had killed dogs in his time—stood a chance against him. His strength was the strength of three, his jaws vicelike, his teeth were sabres, and once an opponent was in his grasp, his powerful hindfeet would rend and tear and scrape it to death.

But how was he to catch his enemy?

Creep read his thoughts. "It'll have to be an ambush of some sort, Captain," he said. "A trick of some kind. You've got to get him to come to you.

Perhaps you could pretend to chum up with him—after all, he doesn't know what you've got in mind—you know, be nice to him."

"Nice?" growled Great Mog. "To him? I'd rather be found dead in a ditch."

"Ah!" said Creep. "Now there you've got something, Captain, there you've got something."

CHAPTER 10

The Dinner Party

It had indeed been a wonderful week on the Bampton–Bush estate. "Kill, kill, kill," Creep had said, and that was the truth, but he should have added, "and eat, eat, eat." For the killing was not for fun, but for food, and what food! No one had ever tasted such a variety of delicacies, for in the old days the Persians had been hand-fed and any outsiders coming in to poach would have ended on the game-keeper's gibbet. Now, thanks to the superb skills of the Mouse Butcher and the expert support of Ecclesiastes and his tribe, every day brought at least two square meals.

The Colonel indeed was beginning to look square. His ribs had vanished, his coat shone, and the old self-satisfied look was back on his flat face. Lady Maud looked positively queenly. True, the red silk bow was tattered still, but the neck which it encircled had filled out, and her loud neighing voice rang all over the Big House as she supervised the preparation and distribution of the dead creatures which her sons carried in.

Ecclesiastes and his many children were in their

seventh heaven. As Giglamps had said at the start, Tom was going to need help in supplying the Bampton-Bushes; and indeed at the end of the week he realised that despite his personal skills he could never have managed without the support of the Vicar's family.

At first he used them as individuals, assigning them various hunting tasks, but he soon realised the virtue of their numbers, setting them in a great half-circle. Their gifts for concealment and absolute stillness, learned in the churchyard, made them ideal ambushers, while he and Di and Ecclesiastes drove game towards them. Rabbit and hare, plump vole and fat fieldmouse, partridge and pheasant even, running head low through the waist-high grass, fled before the Vicar's booming voice and into the jaws of his sons and daughters, and every evening cries of "Simply super!" rang out from the Vicarage as someone brought home something delicious for Genesis and the kittens.

Giglamps did not actually do any hunting. He complained of a touch of rheumatism and of not feeling quite up to the mark. It did not seem to affect his appetite. He struck up quite a friendship with Bertram, and soon the Colonel and Doctor took to spending the evenings together, toying with a drumstick apiece and talking about the old days.

Tom had rapidly become a firm favourite of Lady

Maud's . Any friend of his was thus approved of, and she soon offered the Doctor the use of a spare bedroom in the west wing.

As for the Mouse Butcher himself, life was very sweet. He enjoyed the hunting and the butchering and the magnificent grub. He was extremely comfortable in his now permanent abode in the servants' quarters—the cat-flap at the back of Percy J. Plug's shop had not squeaked for several nights now—and he was happy that all his friends were happy. But most of all, of course, he was head over heels in love with his little huntress Diana. There was, it seemed, no possible cloud on the horizon.

Some days later he sat, at Lady Maud's right paw, on the great dining-room table. There also were the Colonel, the Doctor and the Vicar. It was late in the evening, and the Persian children, tired from the day's hunting, were supposed to be in bed, though several of the boys had sneaked off to court a Truebody, a Goodfellow or a Sturdy girl. Ecclesiastes' family had returned to the Vicarage; Joshua, Psalms, Hosea, Zachariah and all the rest of them, full-fed and happy. (Jonah in particular had had a whale of a time.)

It had been a magnificent meal, a choice of fish or frog's legs followed by a brace of partridge and ending with a variety of savoury dishes—some pheasant eggs, a litter of newborn water-rats and four fat moles.

For a while the grown-ups were silent, and then, politely stifling a belch, Giglamps spoke.

"That really was a monster meal," he said. "Which reminds me. You haven't seen any more of the creature, Tom, have you?"

"Creatchah?" said Lady Maud. "To what creatchah do you refer?"

"The Monster," said Giglamps.

"Monstah?" cried his hostess on a rising note. "Bertie! What does the Doctah mean?"

"It's just a legend, my dear," said the Colonel soothingly. "They say there's a large, er, beast of some kind. Supposed to live in Hobbs' Hole, at the far end of our lands, you know. Never been seen, of course. But there have been some stories. Cats disappearing and so forth."

"Re-mah-kable!" said Lady Maud. "Do you believe this, Vicah?"

Ecclesiastes sat upright, paws together, his usual posture for delivering a sermon. In the twilight the white collar of fur around his throat showed up, clearly.

"My brethren!" he cried. "Let us pray that these tales be not true, lest this fabled giant come forth seeking whom he may devour. Comfort ye with this story, one of many that came to mine ears in the olden days, while mousing during Sunday School. For there was once a human giant, Goliath by name,

who yet was slain by a mere boy. Fear not then," and he turned towards Tom, "for it has come to me, as in a dream, that here is our young David, who shall smite the Philistine of Hobbs' Hole and slay him!"

There was a silence. Tom looked embarrassed, Giglamps amused, the Colonel baffled. Ecclesiastes, all passion spent, jumped down from the table and made his way out through the French windows.

"Re-mah-kable!" said Lady Maud.

CHAPTER 11

Body in the Ditch

Very early the next morning, Tom was fast asleep in the big comfortable armchair in his sitting-room in the servants' quarters.

The first part of the night he had spent cat-napping. Something in the tone of Ecclesiastes' earnest prophecy disturbed him, and when he did fall into a deep sleep the Monster stalked through his dreams. It assumed a variety of shapes, a huge dog-like thing, an enormous bird of prey, a kind of giant weasel. But all the time he knew it was really a cat, and all the time the dreams grew more nightmarish, until at last he was face to face with it, and its great jaws opened wider, wider . . .

The first thing he saw when he opened his eyes was indeed a pair of jaws, but they were delicate white-toothed blue-fringed little jaws, and they closed neatly at the end of a wide yawn.

"Thank goodness you're awake at last," said Diana, staring down at him from the arm of the chair with those huge golden eyes. "I'm bored stiff waiting for you. And you've been jerking about as though you were having a fit. What were you dreaming about? The Hobbs' Hole Monster?"

71

Tom was about to reply "Of course not!", thought of changing it to "What on earth's that?" and finished by mumbling "How . . .?"

"You don't really think I went off to bed last night when Mummy said so, do you? I was under the sideboard. I heard everything the silly old Vicar said."

"Don't you believe in the Monster, then?"

"Of course not, stupid. It's just a story. Anyone would think you were windy, Tom. Monster indeed! I'll tell you what, Mr Mighty Hunter, I'll go down Hobbs' Hole. This very day. After breakfast. By myself. I'm not a scaredy-cat."

A shiver of horror ran down the Mouse Butcher's spine. "You mustn't, Di!" he gasped.

"Mustn't? Mustn't?" said Miss Diana Bampton-Bush, swishing her beautiful plume of a tail. "Who are you to order me about, Mr Tom Plug? The way you talk, anyone would think you were my husband."

She jumped off the arm of the chair and made for the door.

The Mouse Butcher gulped. "There's nothing in the whole wide island I'd like more," he said thickly.

Diana stopped in the doorway. She turned to face him, her eyes dancing, head a little on one side.

"Is that so?" she said. "Well, I'll tell you what, my bold hero. *If* there is a Monster, I'll consider it!"

"You will?"

"On just one further condition."

"What, Di, what?"

"Smite the Philistine of Hobbs' Hole and slay him!" cried Diana in a fair imitation of Ecclesiastes' rolling tones, and she bounced away down the passage.

Tom thought quickly. Suddenly this new life seemed simultaneously wonderful (she had said she would consider) and terrible (he remembered the size of those dreadful footprints). And she had said that she would go down Hobbs' Hole, silly, silly, wonderful tomboy of a kitten that he could not live without and now, it seemed, was fated to die for. He must get there first, go down the Hole, find the . . . find whatever it was.

After all, he told himself, if there is something living in there, maybe it's not so bad, maybe it's just an ordinary cat with big feet, an old cat perhaps, toothless, lonely, glad to see a visitor. Then he could stop Di, tell her "It's just an old hermit, kindly old fellow, wouldn't hurt a fly."

But as he bounded swiftly across the fields in the direction of the marl-pit, he knew in his heart it was not so.

Tom had covered perhaps half the distance when he caught sight of something crossing a gap a hundred yards ahead, something small and low and brown. He thought it was a rabbit or a hare (which was what

Creep had meant him to think) and even in his present haste his hunting instincts would not let him pass by without investigating.

He turned at the gap in the direction in which the thing had gone. There was no sign of a living creature, and Tom, like all cats, hunted mainly by sight. But Tom had a very good nose (as Creep knew), and he soon picked up a scent trail. Not rabbit, not hare, but cat. And a cat, moreover, whose scent he had caught, distantly, fleetingly, several times over the last days.

"It's that little brute Creep," said Tom to himself. "They say he goes to Hobbs' Hole. He should know what lives there. I'll catch the little beast. I'll make him tell me." And nose to ground, he followed swiftly, just as Creep wanted.

The trail led to the end of the field and into a deep ditch. It led along the ditch which wound and twisted and as the scent grew stronger, so Tom pressed forward more eagerly. Rounding a bend, head down, his nose suddenly told him of a second scent, stronger, ranker, and he looked up. Of Creep there was no sign, but right in front of him, not a leap away, an enormous body lay sprawled in the bottom of the ditch.

Every nerve a-jangle, every hair a-tingle, Tom leaped out on to the bank above in one electrified spring. He crouched, ready for anything, fight or flight, he did not know. But there was no flicker of

74

movement below save that the breeze stirred the tabby stripes of ragged patchy fur. Tom crept forward, slowly, inch by inch, the muscles taut under his coal-black coat, until he was right above, and looked down. And the more he looked, the more he became convinced that by a wonderful stroke of luck his horizon had once more become cloudless. For this giant creature, surely, must be the Monster of the marl-pit, and, surely, he was dead.

In fact it was strange he did not smell worse, for it seemed to Tom that he had been dead some time. Bits of him were missing as though scavengers had been at him, bits of ears, and of one foot, and of his tail. He lay half on his back, his forelegs outspread in an attitude of surrender. His head was turned on one side, but Tom could see that his mouth was screwed up, in his death agony he supposed, and that his eye socket was empty.

Tom did not know the saying "Curiosity killed the cat". He crept over the lip of the bank and down into the ditch to have a closer look, and as he bent his head to sniff at the windblown fur, the nightmare from which he had woken not an hour before became reality.

The huge silent motionless shape in the ditch became, in the twinkling of its good eye, a roaring, screaming, snarling Monster!

With fearful strength it clasped the Mouse Butcher

to its mighty chest with forearms like iron bands, its powerful hindfeet pressed against his belly, and its great jaws opened wider, wider . . .

CHAPTER 12

To the Rescue

The Mouse Butcher was not the only occupant of the Big House to have had bad dreams. Diana's brothers' and sisters' sleep was the sleep of youth, deep and undisturbed, while Giglamps, like many elderly people, had lain awake half the night and only dropped off as dawn was breaking. But on the great four-poster-bed in the biggest bedroom, the Colonel mewed pitifully in the grip of his own particular nightmare. Beside him, Lady Maud opened her eyes.

"Bertie!" she said sharply, and nudged him with her nose.

"Mother! Mother! Save me!" cried the Colonel in a high voice, and then, coming to his senses, sat up in bed, a shamed expression on his face.

"I do beg your pardon, my dear," he said. "I fear I woke you."

"No mattah," said Lady Maud, "I dare say you ate too much mole." But she knew and he knew she knew, that it was not that. None of his children, not even the sharp Diana, was aware of the fear that haunted their father. Only his wife knew, and she would have died rather than reveal it to a soul.

Colonel Bertram Bampton-Bush was afraid of mice.

Lady Maud had found out on their honeymoon when the sudden appearance of a mouse had caused Bertram to leap for the safety of the highest chair, where he crouched gibbering with terror. And after she had killed the mouse, wondering, the story had come out. How when he was a tiny kitten, an only child at that, his mother had brought a mouse to the silk-lined basket in which he lay, and for some reason had gone away again. And how the mouse, who was a tough old character still very much alive, had come out of its daze and focused upon the wet black nose of the tiny kitten who was sniffing at it and fastened its sharp teeth in it.

"Mother! Mother! Save me!" the baby had cried, and from that moment on the fear remained. Once the tins of catfood and the choice morsels from Percy J. Plug's shop were no more, the Colonel found that he could eat a dead mouse—it was that or starve—but face a live one he still could not. And in his dreams they harrassed him. All rodents in fact affected him in the same way. If a mouse could hurt his nose, how much more might a rat, or a squirrel, or a stoat? And then birds might peck him, hedgehogs prick him, snakes bite him, wasps sting him. Bertram was in fact a thorough coward, but Lady Maud made sure that no one knew.

"Your fathah," she would say to the children, "is a gentlecat. And gentlecats, unlike the human variety, do *not* hunt."

For all her stiff-necked, aristocratic ways, Lady Maud was only feline, and the excuse about over-eating which she had manufactured for her husband made her think eagerly of breakfast. Tom Plug might be a common or garden cat. But what a difference, she said to herself, he has made to our lives!

She jumped upon the window seat and looked out across the formal garden with its pattern of flower-beds and its pond. At a distance she could see the tribe of Ecclesiastes, their coats of many colours, marching up from the Vicarage in readiness for the day's hunting. Below, making her way across the lawns, was her daughter Diana. It was a still windless morning and the birds were resting after the dawn chorus. Everything was very quiet. Lady Maud broke the silence.

"Di-ah-na!" she called. "Where are you going?"

Diana had decided to set out for Hobbs' Hole straightaway, before her parents woke or the Vicar came or a certain black cat could stop her. She tried to keep the annoyance out of her voice.

"Oh, just for a walk, Mummy," she said, and at that very moment before Lady Maud could even open her mouth to reply, there came to all their ears the most terrible noise that any of them had ever heard in their lives. It came on the still air from the distant fields, a horrible mixture of a roar and a scream with a snarl mixed in, and even at that distance it was so loud that everyone knew one thing for certain. It was the noise of no ordinary creature! In half a minute the lawn was covered in cats as the young Bampton-Bushes poured out of the house and the children of Ecclesiastes arrived at the gallop, while Lady Maud stalked down the steps from the front door followed by a yawning puzzled Giglamps. Only the Colonel did not appear.

For a moment everybody spoke at once, asking questions and arguing, but then the two loudest voices took command.

"Ordah!" cried Lady Maud, and there was order, and then Ecclesiastes' booming tones rang out.

"What is this voice that crieth in the wilderness?" he called. "Can this be the Philistine giant?"

The grown-ups looked at him, remembering the previous evening's talk, and the same thought flashed through all three minds, as the terrible noise swelled up again.

"Where is our young David?"

"Where is Mistah Plug?"

"Where's Tom?" they cried all at once.

As for Diana, her heart was thudding like a trip-hammer at the realisation of the terrible danger into which she had so lightly sent the Mouse Butcher.

"Come on, all of you!" she screamed. "Don't stand there talking! We must help him!" and away she went.

And after her they all ran, blue and tabby, ginger and tortoiseshell, piebald and spotted, a relieving army of cats. Behind the youngsters ran the tall grey figure of Ecclesiastes, behind him Lady Maud, her ragged silk bow a-flutter, and bringing up the rear, the portly shape of the Doctor, puffing and panting at the unaccustomed exercise but with the light of battle in his eyes. The lawns lay empty in the morning sunshine, and beneath the tattered counterpane on the great four-poster-bed the Colonel lay and shivered.

CHAPTER 13

The Discussion

"Och, laddie, laddie, what a mess you're in!" said Giglamps softly, an hour later. They were all gathered in Tom's room when he lay on his side on the hearth-rug. His face was a mask of blood, one ear was slit from tip to base, patches of his black fur had been torn out, and Diana and her mother were licking and cleaning the many wounds upon his body.

"Must have been quite a scrap!" said the Colonel in a hearty voice. "Should like to have lent a paw but I'm afraid I slept through the whole thing! Ha ha!"

"Thank Heaven," said Ecclesiastes gravely, "that we came in time."

After a while they tiptoed away, all but Diana. All that morning and afternoon she lay beside the wounded Butcher and tended to him. She did not waste her breath on apologies or regrets, but worked away to stop the bleeding and start the healing. Tom lay, half asleep, half conscious of that blessed soothing tongue, and by evening, because he was young and very fit, he already felt strong enough to relinquish the first of his nine lives and take up the second. So that when, at dusk, the elders came back

bringing food, he was able to eat a fair meal and to tell them what had happened.

"What I can't understand," said Giglamps, "is how you let yourself get caught by the Monster. I mean, now we've all seen him, we know he's lame. Heavy and strong he may be, but slow and clumsy. I shouldn't have thought he'd have been able to lay a paw on you."

"It was an ambush," said Tom, and he told them how Creep had decoyed him and the Monster had fooled him by shamming dead in the ditch.

"It seems that it was all planned, then?" said Ecclesiastes.

"It must have been," said Tom.

"But why, Plug, why?" asked the Colonel. "I mean attacking a total stranger in that way—well-bred cats simply don't do such a thing."

"You've got it wrong, Colonel," said Giglamps drily. "He's not well-bred, he's hell-bred."

"'The devil is come down unto you, having great wrath, because he knoweth that he hath but a short time'," said Ecclesiastes sonorously.

"I hope he hath," said Giglamps.

"I don't understand it at all," said Tom, answering the Colonel. "All the time we were fighting, it . . . he . . . was shouting at me 'Who cut off my tail? Who killed my mother?'"

"Killed his mothah?" exclaimed Lady Maud.

"I don't imagine you had the time or inclination," said Giglamps, "to ask him what he meant?"

"I hadn't the breath," said Tom. "In fact if you had all come a moment or two later, I'd never have had breath for anything again. You're right Gig, he is slow and awkward because he's crippled in one forefoot. And of course he's got a blind side. But he's so strong, so terribly strong! What with being taken by surprise and held in that grip, I'm only amazed now that he didn't bite my head off in the first few seconds. But I could feel his hindfeet against my stomach and somehow I managed to squirm round to one side, to his blind side as luck would have it. And I got a grip on his neck, under the edge of his jawbone, and I just hung on. At least he couldn't bite me then. I just hung on while he screamed and raved and ripped at me for what seemed a lifetime. And then just at the moment when I knew I couldn't hold on any longer he let go and turned away and I could see you lot coming. Forty-five cats were more than he could face, I'm glad to say. What happened then I don't know, I suppose I must have fainted."

"You did, laddie, you did," said the Doctor. "Not surprising considering the blood you'd lost. What happened then was that he made off back to Hobbs' Hole. Not fast of course, he can't, and we were all close at his heels. But not too close, for every now and then he would whirl round and slash out at the nearest and screech and roar in that terrible voice."

"Ghastly creatchah," said Lady Maud.

"'Resist the devil and he will flee from you'," said Ecclesiastes.

"So he made it back to the hole?" said Diana who had not spoken all this while but only kept her golden eyes on the Mouse Butcher. "I stayed in the ditch with Tom so I didn't see the finish of it."

"Yes," said Giglamps. "He jumped over the edge and we could hear him sliding down and banging and crashing about for a while. And then there was silence."

"Did you see Creep?" Tom asked softly between his teeth. His tail lashed gently.

"Not a sign," said Giglamps. "But from now on nothing will be able to leave or enter the Hole without being observed. The Vicar has set a guard."

"Verily," said Ecclesiastes, "Hobbs' Hole is ringed about. Amos, 1 Samuel, Obadiah, 2 Chronicles and the Song of Solomon hold the first watch—he will sing out if anything is seen."

"Deah Vicah," said Lady Maud, "what should we do without you and your pahfectly splendid youngstahs!"

"Hear, hear!" said the Colonel loudly. "Next time the brute comes out we must be prepared, eh? Give him a taste of his own medicine, what? Ha ha!"

"It's no laughing matter, Daddy," said Diana sharply. "The Monster is mad. He tried to kill Tom, and he'll try again. He must be destroyed. It'll take all of us to do it. Every one of us."

The Colonel gulped.

"Good for you, lassie!" shouted Giglamps.

"We must surround Hobbs' Hole . . ."

"And fall upon him!" boomed Ecclesiastes.

"And murdah the creatchah!" cried Lady Maud.

Painfully the Mouse Butcher pulled himself to his feet.

"Not yet," he said quietly, "not yet. Give me a little more time. I would like to be . . . in at the death."

"Of course," said the Colonel quickly. "You . . . er, that is, we could not do without Plug! And he needs rest! I suggest we all take to our beds."

Diana was the last to leave. She paused in the

doorway. "Tom," she said. "Dear Tom. It was all my fault. Please promise me you'll forget what I said . . . about slaying the Monster by yourself, I mean?"

"Oh, I don't think I could do that," Tom said.

"What d'you mean—you couldn't promise?"

"I mean I couldn't slay him. In single combat. Not judging by today's showing. Could I now?"

But I will, he said to himself when she had gone. I will. Nobody pushes Tom Plug around like that and gets away with it.

CHAPTER 14

Death of a Spy

Creep sat on a high branch in an ash tree. He had run down the ditch, leaping over Great Mog's enormous limp body, and straight up the ash. There he had settled himself comfortably to watch. He expected the Mouse Butcher to be killed. This did not worry him since he had no affection for him. In fact he had no affection for anyone other than himself. He did not hate other cats as Great Mog did. He simply did not care. What he liked was making trouble, and here it came!

Creep sat and watched, his slanting slightly crossed eyes unblinking, while the battle raged and while, just as it seemed as though the Monster would triumph, a multi-coloured army of cats came racing across the fields. He saw Great Mog make off for the Hole, he saw the pursuers harrying him yet not daring to close with him, he saw the little blue female tending to the black cat. He saw the band of rescuers move off again, back towards the Big House, slowly, carefully, the wounded black almost held up amongst them. He saw the ring of sentries posted around the marl-pit. He sat unmoving and waited for the night.

Great Mog was furiously, madly angry. He had been angry most of his lonely bitter life, but never so much as now. To have had that black butcher in his grasp and still not have killed him! To have had to give way to a motley rabble of cats, impudent youngsters mostly, effeminate flat-faced blue creatures some of them, one actually with a bow round its neck! And then, the final insult, to have sentries set around the Hole, his Hole, to spy upon his movements! He considered climbing out to deal with the watchers, catch them, kill them, tear them into tiny pieces! But he knew that he would not be able to catch them, and anyway his neck hurt him very much where that black brute had got a lucky grip on him. Just let one of them come down, just let one! Great Mog tested the wind and took up position, not in his nest in the hollow tree, but right at the edge of the floor of the Hole. His nose told him he was directly below one of the sentries. The breeze brought him his scent, while his own would be wafted away from any cat that dared to climb down. He sat unmoving and waited for the night.

When it was pitch dark Creep slid down the ash tree and made for Hobbs' Hole. He had decided to go into the Hole because he thought he would be safest there. He did not think any other cat on the island would be fool enough to descend into those dark depths which he knew like the back of his paw. Also he was very hungry and there were plenty of little creatures down there, too nimble for the lumbering Monster to catch certainly, but easy meat before his own quick springs. Chiefly he looked forward to teasing the great wild tabby. He imagined himself sitting under the hollow tree, baiting the big ugly beetle-eating, one-eyed crippled mangey smelly freak!

"Good fighter then, is he, Captain? The black one? Give you a hard time, did he? Couldn't manage to finish him off then?"

Creep crawled belly to ground across the last few yards of grass, before the rim of the Hole. He could see the dark shape of the nearest sentry sitting at attention, ears cocked, and he waited for him to turn his head away. When that happened, he slid forward and over the edge. Perhaps it was. because the sentry suddenly looked back, perhaps because the place Creep had chosen was a steep one, perhaps it was simple carelessness, but the fact remained that his descent was not as silent as usual. Sticks snapped, last year's dry leaves crackled, and Great Mog tightened every muscle. One of the sentries is coming down, he thought!

He saw a cat shape in the darkness and his boiling anger lent him strength for the quickest leap of his life. Like a big dog he took the intruder across the small of its back and his furious tusks sank deep.

"Niaouw, Captain! Niaouw!" screamed Creep. And then, more faintly, "Niaouw!"

Mog let the broken spy drop.

"Wretched, rash, intruding fool!" he snarled, but Creep was past hearing. He whispered a final thin "Niaouw!" and then he died.

CHAPTER 15

The Meeting

They held a meeting next morning in Tom's room.
All but the sentries were present. They made Lady
Maud Chair-Persian and, as might be expected, she
got through the business very efficiently. It was
agreed that Hobbs' Hole must be watched night and
day, and here the sum worked out very neatly. The
Vicar had thirty children, not counting the latest
kittens, and five to a watch equalled six watches. Each
cat would therefore do four hours' sentry-go during the
twenty-four. This would still have left plenty of time
for hunting, eating and sleeping, except that Tom felt
that each watch should spend an additional four hours
on stand-by. They could then reinforce the sentries
should the Monster break out, and contain him till the
main body could arrive.

In view of this it was proposed that all the Bampton-
Bushes should be conscripted as hunters rather than
mere porters. Diana, the only experienced one
amongst them, was to be in command. When this
was agreed, the Chair-Persian glanced at her husband.
Pictures of him turning tail before an angry field-

mouse flashed across her mind, but he said nothing and his face was expressionless.

"Much the biggest loss to us at the moment," said Giglamps, "is that of the great skills of our black friend here. We must all do our very best in the hunting field until he is fit again. I shall certainly be out bright and early. The exercise will be good for our figures, eh, Colonel?"

Tom caught Diana's eye, and they twinkled at each other at the thought of the two fat lazy old fellows having to work for their living. Lady Maud waited anxiously for the reply, ready with her instant support should the Colonel begin a string of excuses, but he only said, "Ha ha!"

Finally, Ecclesiastes spoke at great length, with many references to duty, fortitude, and faith, and a rousing reassurance of the certainty of the downfall of the Devil that was in the pit thanks to help that would come from Heaven. It seemed he would go on forever, and there were heads nodding at the back of the room when Lady Maud seized the chance of a brief pause to ask, "Any othah business?"

Tom got to his feet, stiffly. He had woken that morning bruised and sore all over, but even more determined to take on the Monster by himself. He wanted to make sure there would be no random spur-of-the-moment attacks by hot-headed youngsters seeking glory in paw-to-paw combat. He did not care so much for the hurt to his body as to his pride, but he knew he must have time to regain his powers.

"Are we all agreed," he said slowly and deliberately, "that the Monster of Hobbs' Hole must die?"

"Heah! Heah!" cried Lady Maud, and a loud growl of agreement came from all the company of cats.

"Then give me time," said Tom, "to get my strength back, and to think and plan. If he leaves the Hole, shadow him but do not attempt to engage him —he is slow, he cannot catch you. If he stays where he is, then, in due course, we must go down to him." He paused and looked at the ring of faces surrounding him, young faces and old faces, flat ones and sharp ones, blue and tabby, ginger and tortoiseshell, piebald and spotted. There was silence, and for a moment Tom thought that he had lost them, that the fear of the Monster loomed too large, that they would not follow him over the top. Then a familiar voice spoke in an unfamiliar way, not pompously, self-importantly, blusteringly, but in quiet measured tones.

"When the time comes," said the Colonel, "we . . . will . . . go . . . down . . . with . . . you."

And at this there was a great caterwauling of applause, and away they all went to the day's hunting with their heads and their tails and their courage high.

*

Lady Maud and her husband were the last to leave, after making sure that the wounded Butcher was comfortable and well supplied with appetising titbits. Once they were back in their own part of the house, Lady Maud stopped and faced the Colonel. She opened her mouth but for the first time in many years of marriage, nothing came out of it.

"I know, my dear," said Bertram gently, "I know. You're going to say—did I mean it? Will I go when the moment arrives? Or will I . . ." he paused and swallowed, ". . . hide under the counterpane?"

Lady Maud remained silent.

"I did, you know," the Colonel went on, "yesterday. And when I saw you all come back . . . and brave

little Di's face . . . and that gallant fellow Plug . . . and there's me . . ." His voice trailed off.

"There's you where, dearest Bertie?" asked Lady Maud tenderly.

". . . afraid of mice."

For a moment these two aristocatic old Persians stood and looked at one another. Usually Bertram dropped his eyes before his wife's gaze but this time he did not, and in a moment she stepped forward and rubbed her head very gently against his neck.

"Courage," she said quietly, "does not mean feahlessness. Courage means overcoming feah. I believe, Bertie, that you are a brave cat. Are you ready?"

"Ready?" said the Colonel.

"Yes," said Lady Maud Bampton-Bush briskly. "Ready to come with me to the stables. Where I will find you a mouse. And you will kill it."

CHAPTER 16

Skirmishes

Great Mog sat in his nest in the hollow tree and stared out with his one baleful eye. The hot weather was breaking up and there was thunder about. Round the rim of the Hole the sentries sat, disciplined and watchful as ever.

Two weeks had passed since the fight with Tom, and in the world of the island outside the marl-pit there was plenty going on. Inside, almost the only movement was that of the wild things who lived there. Once a day perhaps, the Monster would climb down for a drink and whatever he could find to eat— unfledged birds dropped from the trees, a litter of baby mice, mouthfuls to keep him going—but mostly he sat and cursed. He cursed the steel trap that had crippled his foot, he cursed the shot-gun pellets that had robbed him of an eye, he cursed all the creatures —men, dogs, cats—that had caused him injuries over the years. Especially he cursed Percy J. Plug, and most especially his cat. Another minute, he swore, and I would have killed him. Perhaps because he could not get at it to clean it, the bite under his jaw had gone septic, and he cursed at the pain of it.

On a sudden impulse he jumped out of the hollow tree, hopped three-legged across the floor of the pit past the bones of Creep, picked clean by scavengers, and began to climb the steep side.

He was hoping to slip past the sentries but long before he had reached the top, the nearest one—it was Jeremiah—heard him and yowled a warning to the others who ran from their posts to join him.

"Oh dear, oh dear," groaned Jeremiah, "just look what the dog brought in."

Great Mog snarled furiously and slashed out with his good forepaw, but the nimble young Vicarage cats danced easily out of danger. Two of them, Ruth and Esther, cheeky ginger girls, burst into fits of giggles at his clumsy rushes, and soon there were ten of Ecclesiastes' children, for the quarter-guard came rushing up to join the watch, surrounding the maddened Monster. And how they baited him!

"It's enough to make a cat laugh!" shouted Proverbs.

"How many lives have you lost?" yelled Numbers. "More than nine by the look of you!"

"Just look what's come out of the lion's den!" cried Daniel. "Is it a pussy or a bow-wow, what's your verdict, Judges?" And they whirled around in a dizzy circle, shouting rude words that would have horrified their reverend father.

Soon they became too bold and first one and then

another, coming too close, felt the weight of the Monster's slashing paw-stroke and were sent spinning away, squealing with pain. At this, the rest drew back and stopped their catcalling, but they still ringed him about, and Great Mog realised there was no point in going on. He turned his heavy head and looked at them in turn as if to memorise their faces. Then he wheeled and dropped back down into the Hole.

When the quarter-guard came excitedly into Tom's room, it was a very different animal to whom they made their report from the battered bloodstained creature of two weeks ago. Though he would always carry the split ear as a memento, his wounds had completely healed. He had had the best of care, for at Ecclesiastes' suggestion, Genesis had come up daily from the Vicarage to attend to him. The most motherly of creatures, she had spoiled and fussed over him in her blunt hearty way, selecting from the larder next door the best of everything the hunters brought in.

"Brekky!" she would cry. "Simply super grub today! Tuck in!" And then, "Seconds! Come on! Find a corner! That's right! Good boy! Jolly well done!" until he was full to bursting.

She always brought the seven small kittens with her, and at first they sat in a row on an old sofa opposite Tom's chair, round-eyed with wonder at the sight of the coal-black Butcher with his torn ear who gazed at them with his green eyes. But after a day or two they began to play, first among themselves, jumping and wrestling and batting at one another in fierce mock-fights; and soon the bravest climbed on to Tom's chair and patted tentatively at his nose.

"Ezekiel!" cried Genesis, coming in from the larder with a fresh-plucked bird. "Jolly well stop that, my lad! Mr Plug doesn't want to be bothered!" But Tom said that he did, and that he liked kittens, and anyway it was time for a little exercise.

And so he built up, to a point where "a little exercise" was a wild daily free-for-all while stout Genesis looked affectionately on. It was wonderful training for the little ones and the best possible way

for Tom to rebuild his speed and timing, as he leaped, twirled, somersaulted and catapulted about the little sitting-room in the servants' quarters of the Big House. It was seven against one, and everybody enjoyed it enormously.

Afterwards, when they lay and panted for breath, Tom would look fondly at his new small friends and think how nice it would be one day, to have kittens of his own. And he would half close his eyes, so that the stout tabby figure of the Vicar's wife became beautiful and slender and blue, and the rolypoly shapes on the carpet turned blue also—or were a couple of them black?

Dear little things, he thought, who would dream of harming them? And then he sat up sharply, eyes narrowed, tail swishing, for he knew who would! No creature on the island was safe while that crazy giant could come out of the Hole. He must die, thought Tom, and I must be the one to kill him. And to do it I must be, not just as fast on my feet as I used to be, but faster, faster! And off he would go again with his seven sparring partners.

In fact, by the day when the quarter-guard came tumbling in with their news, Tom was almost fighting fit again.

CHAPTER 17

Shoulder to Shoulder

As for the rest, things had gone well. Diana, with Ecclesiastes' help, had drilled her brothers and sisters into passable performers, and at the end of each day's hunting, when the Vicar and those of his family not on duty had gone home, she and Tom would spend the evening together. She would tell him all that had happened, and he would lie and rest and gaze at her, purring his happiness.

The Doctor, she told him, was proving an excellent provider.

"What, dear old Gig?" said Tom in amazement. "Running about, catching things?"

"Not exactly running," said Diana. "Thing is, he found the fish-pond, the very first day. And I don't know exactly what happened, whether he was lying down having a drink . . ."

"Tired out after walking a hundred yards," interrupted Tom.

". . . or what, but anyway apparently he caught a fish. Only a little one at first, but soon he was catching the big ones."

"That explains it," said Tom. "The Vicar's wife brought me in a whopper yesterday. I thought perhaps your father was pulling them out."

"I don't know what's come over Daddy," said Diana. "We were always brought up to believe that gentlecats didn't hunt—oh sorry, Tom, I wasn't thinking . . ."

"That's all right," Tom said, "go on."

"Well, I saw Mummy and Daddy this morning, in the stables, that's where they've mostly been—and Daddy was actually sharpening his claws on a doorpost and his beard was covered in blood."

The Colonel had indeed conquered his old fear, thanks to his newfound determination and the help of his wife. Lady Maud had started him very gently, on an extremely small mouse whose back she had secretly broken. Shaking like a leaf, his eyes tight shut, Bertram had managed to open his mouth and close it again upon the wretch. The mouse died and Bertram ate it warm and juicy. The blood of his ancestors began to stir and the next mouse his wife

turned out for him, he actually pursued and caught. By the end of the two weeks when Diana saw him, he was on to rats and loving every minute of it.

That evening, Tom came into the drawing-room where the Bampton-Bushes were resting after the day's work and a good supper. The weather had broken and the rain was drumming on the windows.

"Ah, Plug!" cried the Colonel heartily. "How are you? Ready for action?"

"Yes, thank you Colonel," Tom said. "That's what I've come to see you about."

"Are you reahly bettah, Tom?" said Lady Maud. She no longer called him "Mistah Plug" and her harsh voice was almost tender.

"Yes, I'm quite fit again, Lady Maud," said Tom. Time I stopped saying "my lady", he thought, if she's going to be my mother-in-law. And that's a big "if". I've got to kill the Monster first.

So he told them about the skirmish and how two of the Vicar's children had been roughed up by the Monster.

"It's time we moved in on him," he said. "Before anyone else gets hurt. I think we should attack at dawn."

So a runner was sent to the Vicarage to summon Ecclesiastes, and another to the West Wing to wake the snoozing Doctor, and the simple plan was agreed.

"We'll encircle the Hole," said Tom, "at first light.

And then we'll go down into it, every one of us, and tighten the circle, bit by bit, searching every tree and bush and thicket, till we have him trapped in the very centre."

It rained most of the night, but the day dawned clear, and the rising sun shone brightly upon the faces of the approaching army. They ringed Hobbs' Hole and at a loud yowl from Tom they went over the top and down the steep sides. Their hearts were in their mouths, but they had faith in each other and in their leader, the Mouse Butcher. They moved forward steadily, tightening the noose, until at last they stood, shoulder to shoulder, around a big hollow tree in the very centre of the marl-pit. On its bark were the Monster's claw-marks and inside it his nest, and all about it his rank scent. But of Great Mog himself there was no sign!

CHAPTER 18

Break Out, Break In

When Great Mog had retreated before the taunting of the Vicar's children, he had made his way, angry and frustrated, back to the hollow tree. A few big drops of rain fell through the canopy of leaves as he pushed his way across the floor of the pit, and the germ of an idea came into his brain. He sat in his nest thinking hard, so hard that he did not take any notice of the voices of the watchers above as they settled back at their sentry posts after all the excitement. By the time the next relief had arrived and the guard had been changed, he had made a plan.

He needed three things: darkness, heavy rain, and a convenient tree. For the first two he must wait, but he went looking for the third. The new watch could hear him as he moved around the outside of the bed of the Hole, but they could see nothing below through the thick greenery.

Great Mog stopped at the bottom of several trees, peering upwards with his one eye. One or two he climbed a short way, the better to see, though making sure he was not in view from above. At last he seemed to find what he wanted, and he went back to his nest.

The hours passed, darkness fell, and the watch above changed again. Some while before, the rain had started, and now it was coming down in earnest, beating and splashing on the thick leafiness of Hobbs' Hole, drowning every noise. Great Mog made his way to the tree he had chosen and began to climb. It was a slow business, for the tree was tall and the climber clumsy, but at last, he found what he had hoped for. Almost level with the top of the pit, a branch stuck out towards the edge of it. He crept along it. Now he only needed a bit of luck, and he got it. He was midway between two sentries. Lashed by the rain, deafened by it, their noses useless because of it, they crouched miserably and saw nothing at all when Great Mog took one huge leap from the end of the branch. He landed safely and was gone into the wet black night.

Once he was well clear of the Hole, he looked for some shelter. He needed to rest and to think. He swerved away to one side, for he did not want to be on the route between the Hole and the Big House, and after a while he found an old tumble-down shed in the corner of a field. There was some fusty straw inside, and amongst it he found a nest of baby rats and bolted them. He settled down to think again. How could he get the Mouse Butcher alone? His eye flashed

and his stump twitched at the thought—this time he would make no mistake. But the odds were so heavy against him—every cat his enemy—no Creep to spy out the lie of the land for him—once they found him they would drive him back—he couldn't fight them all. They would drive him back into the Hole where they could sit and look down on him.

If only he could find somewhere to sit and look down on *them*, somewhere high, perhaps with a narrow approach where they could only come at him one at a time. Five cats or fifty, he would take them all on. Just let the black one come first.

Great Mog slept fitfully for a little while and then moved on. The rain had stopped and a brilliant moon had come from behind the clouds. By its light he could see, below and to his right, a cluster of wet roofs that he knew must be the village and soon he made out the loom of a large building not far in front of him. Is that the Big House? he thought, and didn't have to wait long for the answer.

In the half-light of dawn, he saw a dozen or more blue cats, one of them with that stupid ribbon round its neck, come out of the front door of this building and down a flight of steps on to the grass in front. After them, yawning, came a fat old ginger cat with markings like spectacles round its eyes. And coming up the drive from the direction of the village marched a tall grey cat with a band of white fur round its throat, leading a pack of thirty others of many colours. Lastly—how Great Mog growled in his throat at the sight—a coal black figure bounded lightly down the steps and pushed through the throng, and away they all went towards Hobbs' Hole.

As the great wild tabby began to move towards the now deserted house, the first rays of the sun caught the topmost part of it, a square turretted tower. It had a round design on the front of it, and above that, on either side, a tall wooden pole and a sharp metal spike.

Great Mog knew nothing of clock-towers, or flag-staffs, or lightning conductors. But what he did know when he saw it was a high place, with a narrow approach. He limped quickly forward to the nearest wall, thickly covered with ivy, and began to climb.

CHAPTER 19

The Fight

Half an hour later the army came back. Tom had left a couple of look-outs by the Hole in case the Monster should return but the rest were gathered on the lawns. There was a great sense of anti-climax. Giglamps voiced the general feeling.

"What a letdown!" he said. "At least we've known exactly where he was these last two weeks. Now he could be anywhere."

"We must find him," said Tom. "We must forget about the hunting today and split up and comb the island. We'll divide into four patrols. Vicar, will you take one, and search the village? Tell your wife to keep the kittens in a place of safety. I want the other three to take the farms, Truebody's, Goodfellow's and Sturdy's. Lady Maud, will you lead one, and the Colonel and Gig the others? Get the farm cats to help. Warn them what we're up against."

"What about me then?" said Diana pettishly. "Why can't I lead a patrol? I've been organising the hunting, haven't I?"

"I've got a special task for you," Tom said. Where

you'll be out of danger, he thought. I'm not running any risks with you.

Within a short time the older cats had split the army into four and were moving off to their various areas. Ecclesiastes was the last to go, and first he came up to Tom and looked down at him.

"Where will you go, my friend?" he said.

"I'm going to patrol around this house," said Tom. He felt in his bones that the Monster would come to the Big House. Then he would fight him, alone.

"Goodbye then, young David," said Ecclesiastes with a quizzical look, "and good luck should Goliath come."

I may need more than luck, said Tom to himself, but again the Vicar seemed to read his thoughts.

"I believe that help will come to you—from on high," said Ecclesiastes gravely, and he turned and led his troops away.

"What's this special task then?" said Diana when they were alone.

"Look-out," said Tom. "I'm going to be going round the house and buildings here, but I can't see all round. And I don't want him to jump me if he should come. But if you get on the highest point you can see everywhere for a long way, and give me warning."

"The clock-tower?" said Diana quickly.

"Exactly," said Tom.

He watched her bouncing up the flight of steps, heard her pattering across the hall, imagined her climbing the broad staircase to the first floor. Then she would run along the window-lined corridor, up the narrow wooden stairs to the attics, in one of which there was a sky-light open. One jump on to a table, a second on to the top of a chest-of-drawers, the third through the skylight and out on to the tiles— they had done it so often hunting birds on the roof. Lastly—she must be there by now—she would climb the little spiral of stone steps that led up inside the clock-tower.

Tom walked out on to the lawns and turned to look up, and at that very instant there came from the tower a squeal of terror and a roar of frustrated anger, and his blood ran cold as he recognised both voices. For a split second he could not move a muscle. Then, like a starting-gun, there came a great crack of thunder from the heavens above, and the Mouse Butcher shot away to the rescue like a black bullet.

By the time he reached the roof the rain was pouring down, but he could hear Diana's voice above the noise of it and suddenly he saw her. She had somehow climbed the flagpole and was crouched precariously on the round wooden boss at the top of it.

"Tom! Tom!" she screamed. "He's up here! The Monster's up here!"

And from the tower there came a thunderous

rolling growl to mingle with the noise of the storm.

"I'm coming!" yelled Tom.

"No, Tom. No!" she squealed. "Get the rest! Get help! I'm all right up here, he can't get up this pole, he's tried. He's too heavy and clumsy. But you'll never make it up the spiral staircase, it's too narrow, he's waiting at the top! Please get help! Please Tom, don't try to fight him by yourself!"

But that's just what I want to do, thought Tom grimly. And anyway, if we had a hundred cats here they would still have to come at him one at a time.

The thunder was banging all around now and the air was charged with electricity. A flash of lightning lit up the clock-face above him. It had stopped, all those moons ago, at a quarter to three. Tom went back a few paces, then turned, and ran, and leapt. He landed on the horizontal bar of the big hand for an instant, hurled himself upward, and caught the top of the wall with his forepaws. He kicked desperately against the stone with his hindfeet and somehow hauled himself up.

Beside him was the metal spike of the lightning conductor and opposite him the white wooden flag-pole with Diana perched on high. Below him was the top of the tower, a small open area perhaps ten feet square. And at one side of it, by the low black hole that was the exit from the staircase, crouched the Monster. His mangey tabby coat was dark with rain, the remains of his ears were flat back against his huge head, and his stump of a tail twitched. He was facing directly away from Tom.

Dozens of times during his convalescence Tom had imagined his second meeting with the Monster, had fought him in his mind in dozens of different ways in dozens of different places, but always he knew that this time he must keep clear of those hugging forearms and those rending hindfeet and those gaping jaws. This time he must get behind him somehow, surprise him, leap on his back, dig in, hang on, bite deep. There would never be a better chance. Tom jumped.

Though Tom was only half his weight Great Mog was knocked sprawling. His feet splayed out, his jaw hit the ground hard, and the old wound from the first fight opened up again. Just beside it, sharp teeth bit into the scruff of his neck and sharp claws gripped his back. Somehow he managed to turn his head enough to focus his one eye on his attacker. When he saw it was the black cat, Great Mog went mad!

He shot straight up in the air as if he was carrying nothing heavier than a fly and then began to leap and buck and turn and twist just as a wild horse tries to dislodge its rider. And the rider held on desperately, teeth locked, claws holding tight. And directly above them now the storm raged, so close that thunderclap followed on lightning flash with hardly any interval.

It was the confined space that was to be Tom's undoing. If the fight had been in the open country, he might have been able to stick on; but when Great Mog could not shift him, he tried other tactics. He

began to hurl himself sideways at the rough stone walls of the tower top, hoping to brush Tom off, or knock him off, or wind him so that he would let go.

Crash! Bash! Tom was bruised and battered as the crazy Monster threw himself about, but he dared not let go his grip. He realised that his speed and foot-work would count for nothing in such a small area, but the Monster's frenzied strength seemed to grow, while his own was ebbing away.

From the corner of his eye he saw Diana scrambling backwards down the flagpole and to his horror he realised that she was going to join in the fight. Instinctively he opened his mouth to shout, "No, Di! No!" And as Great Mog felt his grip relax he gave one mighty twirling somersault and threw the Mouse Butcher from his back. All the breath was knocked out of Tom's body, and he could only watch as the Monster turned on Diana. Brave as a lioness, she came spitting and clawing at him, and as she came, Great Mog sat back on his heels and hit her one tremendous blow with his good paw, knock-ing her clean through the low stone doorway and out of sight down the stairs. Then he turned and faced Tom.

For a moment neither moved, while the lightning flashed, nearer it seemed, and the thunder roared louder. Tom was fighting to get his breath back, and as for Great Mog, he was quite simply savouring the situation. Above his distorted mouth the one eye gleamed and the stump of his tail twitched slowly, slowly. The black cat was done for!

Tom dived under the leap as Great Mog came for him and wheeled to face him again from the other side of the tower top. He did not know if Diana was dead or alive. He did not see how he himself was to come out of this living. He only knew he would not cut and run. He would fight to the death. Crack! went another thunderclap. Behind him, as he waited, there rose the steel spike of the lightning conductor, and behind the crouching Monster opposite, the wooden flagstaff.

Thoughts rushed through Tom's brain. I can't just keep dodging him. I must hit back, cripple him somehow, slow him down, get him off balance, tip him over the edge perhaps. And this time he did not dive beneath the spring, but, waiting until the last instant, leapt aside, and, as the Monster landed struck with all his strength at the one good eye. Momentarily blinded, Great Mog reared upon his hindlegs with a scream of fury, and groping sightlessly to clutch his enemy with those great hugging forearms, embraced the lightning conductor. And even as he did so, there came from on high one colossal zig-zagging airsplitting thunderbolt that homed upon the steel spike like a missile. From the rocking tower one last great cry rang out, from the skies one last great clap, and it was all over. Only a horrid smell of singed fur told the tale.

When Tom came to his senses, it was to see the dazed figure of Diana emerging from the head of the stairs.

"Are you all right?" they both cried and, "Yes, yes, are you?" and, "Thank Heaven!"

"Thank Heaven indeed!" boomed the familiar voice of Ecclesiastes. Searching the church tower, the Vicar had seen from that high place the lightning strike the other.

"Did I not tell you so, Tom?" he said. "For it is written 'Thou shalt heap coals of fire upon his head'." And, silently now, they all moved away, down the steps and back through the skylight into the familiar comfort of the Big House.

The storm was gone, the rain had ceased, the wind fallen, and presently the sun came out and shone down upon the great spread-eagled body on the top of the clock-tower. In his death, as in his life, Great Mog was all alone.

CHAPTER 20

Paradise Regained

Another twelve moons had waxed and waned, and once again Tom Plug was lying upon the bare marble slab in the window of his empty shop, gazing down the deserted village street. Opposite him lay his even more elderly friend, Giglamps Macdonald. The scene outside would have appeared ruinous to human eyes, for the winter storms had done much damage to men's handiwork. Many of the houses were roofless now, many of their windows broken by the thrashing branches of overgrown trees. Percy J. Plug's name was washed out from the shop-front and behind the door his blue-striped apron and straw hat were dusty ruins.

But the humans never had come back, and the cats no longer thought of them. In the early days air-machines had quite often been seen, passing high above the island, but not for a long time now.

"How time flies," said Tom reflectively. He was as black and sleek and hard as ever. Only the deep-split ear told its tale.

"Aye, it does, it does, laddie," said the Doctor yawning. "None of us are getting any younger. Only a wee bit stouter," and he fell to cleaning the fur on his ample stomach.

"One or two old faces gone, in the village, I notice," mused Tom.

"Och, there's enough new ones coming along," laughed the Doctor. "You've done your share there! That first lot of yours and Diana's—why, I sometimes wonder how I'm to get a moment's rest. It's 'Take us hunting, Uncle Gig. Tell us a story, Uncle Gig', all day long. Why, d'you know, the other day they wanted me to take 'em down Hobbs' Hole!"

"Did you?"

"Well no, it's a bit steep for me at my time of life, but I let them play about there for a bit. Brought back some memories."

There was a silence. By common consent no one ever spoke of the clock-tower. Tom had managed to knock out the catch that held the skylight open when they came down that day, and it slammed shut forever.

"You're very good with them, Gig," Tom said. "Diana really appreciates it now she's got the second lot on her paws."

"It's a great pleasure to me, Tom, you know that," said Giglamps. "Just don't go trying to beat the Vicar. I was over there the other day and they're on to New Testament names now." He mimicked Genesis' hearty tones. "Jolly little lot, Doctor. Four little boys.

Matthew, Mark, Luke and John! Simply super!"

"No, I don't think we'll ever do that," said Tom. "Though their grandparents wouldn't object, they don't half spoil this lot. Did I ever tell you, when our first kittens were born, Bertram wanted to kill the peacock for a feast of celebration. Bloodthirsty old chap my father-in-law is nowadays. I wouldn't have minded—that bird's been on my mind since we first met—but Lady Maud wasn't having any."

He took his turn at imitation. "'Bertie! Tom! Di-*ah*-na!'" he bawled. "'The peacock is the emblem of the Royal House of Pershah! You will do no such thing evah!' So we didn't."

They lay quietly on the sunlit slab for a while, and then the Doctor got up and stretched himself.

"Well laddie, I must be going," he said. "I promised to teach your older lot fishing. They'll be waiting up at the Big House. Anyway, Mrs Plug and the latest little Plugs will be back soon and wanting their tea. Why don't you and Diana come up to my place one evening and have some supper?"

What you mean, my dear old friend, thought Tom, is why don't I bring some supper.

"What I mean is," said Giglamps with a twinkle, "why don't you bring some supper?" and he jumped heavily off the slab and forced his way out through the cat-flap.

And as the Mouse Butcher lay staring out of the

window of his shop with his sharp green eyes, he saw at the bottom of the village street, eight figures approaching. Seven were roly-poly figures, tumbling and playing about the empty dusty road, five of them blue and two of them coal-black. But the eighth one was the most beautiful creature Tom had ever seen. She had the flattest face, the blackest nose, the dearest little whiskers, the most glorious golden eyes, and her coat—her long soft exquisite coat—was the most wonderful shade of the most wonderful blue that Tom could possibly have imagined in all the world, a world turned once again into Paradise.

He stood up and they all came running.